Whether it's real or imagined, most teenagers feel hassled at home. But some actually get kicked around –and often they kick back. Such is the story of Denise.

Maybe you can identify with Denise. You've sampled some of the "answers" that are out there and still come out hurting. Now read about the real answer that gave Denise a whole new start in life. Maybe it's exactly what you, too, have been looking for all along.

BY John Benton

Denise

John Benton

Fleming H. Revell Company
Old Tappan, New Jersey

ISBN: 0-8007-8451-0
A New Hope Book
Copyright © 1983 by John Benton
All rights reserved
Printed in the United States of America
This is an original New Hope Book, published by New Hope Books, a division of Fleming H. Revell Company, Old Tappan, New Jersey.

Denise

1

I jumped off the school bus but waited until it had driven off before heading up the path to our house. Ever since I could remember I'd been embarrassed by the way my family lived. I hated for the bus to stop there and for the rest of the kids to know this was where I lived. The place needed painting, and the junked cars in the yard certainly didn't add to its appearance.

Mom kept fussing about the cars, but Dad, who was a mechanic, kept insisting that one day he'd need some of the parts off of those junkers. And so they stayed.

The front steps creaked as I walked up them, carefully avoiding the rotted board on the third step. Since my hands were full of books, I kicked open the front door.

Before I could even get inside I heard it: "Denise? Is that you?"

Whom did she expect? And why couldn't she at least let me get inside the door before she started yelling? I recognized the tone of voice. It meant she was mad about something. So what else was new? I never could please that woman, no matter how hard I tried.

Ignoring her, I walked into the living room and dropped my books on the hardwood floor—just for effect.

The bang and clatter brought another scream: "Denise? Is that you?"

Without a word I flipped on the TV and plopped into a chair. I hated school, and I hadn't done too well on a couple of major tests today. Maybe an afternoon rerun would help me forget. . . .

But over the noise of the TV I could hear Mom's heavy footsteps coming from the kitchen. She stationed herself between me and the TV set and yelled, "Young lady, when I ask you something, I expect you to answer me!"

I sat there staring belligerently. Even after all the times I'd seen her, I never quite got over the shock. She had no trouble blocking my view of the TV; she could block anything! My mom was fat, sloppy, and ugly all rolled up into one big package. I don't think the woman had done one honest hour's work in her lifetime. All the time we three kids were in school, she sat around eating candy and watching the soaps. And she expected us to clean the house, do the dishes, and anything else that needed to be done. Her only contribution was to fix the meals, and I think that was because she could stuff her face while she was preparing the food. There was no doubt about it; my mom loved food—especially junk food.

Her screams brought me back to the moment. "Young lady, I want you to come with me," she announced. "I want to show you something."

"In a minute," I said. That usually satisfied her.

Sometimes she even forgot she wanted something done. Sometimes she made my brother or sister do it—but not too often.

This time, however, she wasn't about to be put off. First I heard her curse. Then I saw her heading toward me. I tried to get out of the way, but I just wasn't fast enough. Her hand grabbed my hair and gave a big jerk.

The torrent of hate for her, bottled up inside me, came loose when she did that. I could stand spankings and lectures, but I never could stand it when she pulled my hair. I think she knew it and did it deliberately to bait me.

She had jerked me to my feet, and I doubled my fist and let her have it right in the gut. I should have known it was next to impossible to penetrate all that flab. She let out an "Oof!" and backhanded me across the face. At the same time she jerked even harder on my hair and spun me around. I felt my feet sliding out from under me, and I landed hard on the floor. But that wasn't all. As I hit the floor, she kicked me with all her might— right in my side!

"You beast!" she screamed. "You have never had any respect for your mother! Now when I say something to you, I expect a civil answer. Is that asking too much from a prima donna?"

I looked up at the monster standing over me. At that moment I was ready to do anything I could to hurt her in any way I could. But I knew I was no match for her. I'd better cool it, or I'd have some broken ribs!

"I'm sorry," I said lamely. "I didn't hear you."

"Don't lie to me!" she fumed. "You've got good ears. You heard me. You just didn't feel like answering."

"I was concentrating on the story on TV."

"More lies!" She spit out the words, showing her obvious contempt for my excuse.

"Now get up this minute and come with me!" she ordered. "I've got something I want you to see."

What would it be this time? Whenever I came home from school, it was something. She was always cursing, always yelling. And almost every day I got slapped around. One of these days I'd show her. I'd take off.

With a disgusted "What is it this time?" I slowly got up and started wobbling toward the kitchen. My side was killing me, but I decided not to give her the satisfaction of knowing how much it hurt.

She then grabbed my elbow, but I jerked away with a "Get your filthy hands off me!"

I could see her fist clench, so I took off for the kitchen as fast as I could, under the circumstances.

The kitchen was filthy—just like always. She enjoyed cooking, but cleaning up afterward wasn't her bag. But what was bugging her? This was how the kitchen usually looked.

She pointed toward the kitchen table and demanded, "Is that your cereal bowl?"

I looked at her, puzzled. What was she getting at?

Then she pointed at the kitchen sink and said loudly, "Did you take that carton of milk out of the refrigerator this morning?"

I shrugged. Sometimes I remembered to put the milk back in the refrigerator; sometimes I didn't. It bothered me that I was becoming so much like my sloppy mother.

I walked over, grabbed the carton, held it under my nose, and took a deep breath. "There's nothing wrong with this milk," I announced. "So maybe it's a little warm. What's the big deal? It's a little warm when it comes from the cows."

"That milk is sour from being left out all day!" she shouted.

To prove her wrong, I lifted the carton to my lips and took a swallow. "It's not sour!" I shouted back.

Mother snatched the carton out of my hand and yelled, "How dare you get your filthy germs all over the pouring spout! Don't you know that's a terrible thing to do?"

Mother was concerned about germs? If she were, she ought to start cleaning up this pigpen we lived in!

"Look, I just tasted the milk to prove it wasn't sour," I said.

"You think you're pretty cute, don't you?" she answered sarcastically. "Someday I'm going to beat that out of you!"

I got her message. I should have put the milk away and washed my dish. So I started back to the TV.

"Just a minute, young lady. I'm not through with you yet."

"Now what?" I asked disgustedly.

"Come with me!"

She walked by me and started upstairs, motioning for me to follow. When I realized she was heading into the room I shared with Dagmar, my eighteen-year-old sister, I knew I was in trouble. Dagmar kept her half of the room reasonably neat. My half? Well, that was another story.

Mom paused as she passed the bathroom and pointed. "Take a look in there."

I looked. It seemed the same as usual—cluttered sink, towels strewn on the floor, my pajamas right where I had stepped out of them.

"What's wrong?" I asked. "It looks normal to me."

"Don't get smart, Denise. From now on you pick up your clothes and towels. Do you hear me?"

"What's the big deal?" I demanded. "How come all of a sudden we are overcome with a desire for cleanliness?"

She grabbed my arm and started digging her fingernails into it. The more I tried to jerk away, the harder she dug. Realizing it was useless to resist, I relaxed.

"It's about time a sixteen-year-old girl learned to pick up after herself," she told me. "And I mean to see that you start doing it. From now on before you leave for school, you are to pick up your clothes, wash out your cereal bowl, and put the milk back in the refrigerator. Is that clear?"

Her attitude puzzled me, and I looked at her quizzically. She didn't look any different. Her hair hadn't been combed all day, and her dress had food spots all over it. What caused the sudden big deal about cleanliness?

"Look, Mom, I'll do it," I said. "But please tell me why all of a sudden we have these new rules?"

Still tightly gripping my arm, she replied, "I am getting sick and tired of all your messes, Denise. So I decided you were going to have to change your ways."

I couldn't believe this! If I had to change my ways, would everybody else? Did that include my kid brother, Philip? His room was an unmitigated disaster. Sure, he was only ten, but he had absolutely no idea what the words *cleanliness* and *tidiness* meant! Dagmar was a little better than I was, but she had the habit of piling her clothes on top of the dresser. Most of the time it looked like Mount Saint Helens—ready to blow its top!

"I'll try to do better," I told her. "But I understand this will mean that Philip does better, Dagmar does better, and you do better too."

"You smart little thing!" she exploded, pushing me into the wall. "I'm the one who gives the orders in this house. I decide who is going to do what and when. So you do as I say, or you are going to find yourself in deep trouble!"

I would have bolted for the door, but she was smack in the middle of it. No way could I get by.

Then we heard the front door slam and Philip yell, "Hey, Ma, are you home?"

"Yes, darling," she called back in a syrupy-sweet voice.

I bristled. She treated him as though he was the dearest, sweetest thing on the earth, and she treated me like I was the dirt beneath her feet. Why couldn't she love me too? Why didn't she treat me at least as nicely as she did her few friends?

"I'm starved!" Philip yelled. "Can you fix me a pea-nut-butter-and-jelly sandwich?"

My kid brother was at that age when he had a bot-tomless pit for a stomach. But wasn't he old enough to be able to fix his own sandwich?

"Yes, darling, I'll be right down," Mother called.

Still brooding over the difference in the way she treated the two of us, I followed Mother down the stairs. Maybe now I could watch TV.

Philip jumped out of a hiding place to try to scare me as I got to the bottom of the steps. I punched him play-fully and asked, "Hey, Phil, how'd it go today?"

"Great! Just great!" he responded. "I got an *A* on that big history test."

He got an *A*, and I flunked two tests today. I don't know how he did it. He never seemed to spend much time studying. For that matter, neither did Dagmar. But both of them made good grades. I guess I must have been in hiding when the brains were passed out in my family.

My conversation with Philip made Mother realize I was right behind her. She turned, pointed upstairs, and said, "You've got some things to do up there, young lady. Now go do them. And then report to me in the kitchen!"

My side hurt worse as I walked up the stairs again. Maybe she had broken one of my ribs this time!

I rather quickly picked up my things in the bathroom and then headed for my bedroom. As I started straightening it, I turned around and saw Dagmar enter.

"Hey, sis, I don't know if she's hit you yet or not, but the old lady's on a cleanliness binge."

"Mom? I don't believe it!" Dagmar said, laughing. "If she's talking about cleanliness, she's probably drunk!"

"You really think so?" I queried. "I didn't smell—"

"No, she's not drunk," Dagmar continued, laughing again. "But I do know she is really ticked off about something. I heard her reaming you out."

Dagmar was counting the weeks until she'd be out of high school. She was already preparing to move out right after graduation. We had talked about the possibility of my going with her, but I sure didn't want that word to get around.

"Did you know she yanked my hair and kicked me in the ribs when we were downstairs?" I asked.

"No, but I heard her up here, and she sure sounded mad. How come she's on your case constantly?"

So Dagmar had noticed it too! Why was Mother always mad at me but not at Philip and Dagmar?

I started back downstairs, carrying my dirty clothes which I stuffed into a laundry basket on the back stairs. Then I headed back to watch TV.

No sooner had I gotten absorbed in the new program than Mother marched in, shouting, "Denise, you get up right now and start picking things up around here."

She didn't have to tell me twice. I was still hurting from her beating, and I didn't want to be on the receiving end of more kicks or slaps or pulled hair.

As I looked around the living room, I hardly knew where to start. I figured the books I had dropped would be one possibility. Then I could pick up some magazines that were strewn around the floor.

I had started the task when Philip walked through, putting on his baseball glove.

"Hey, brother, give me a hand, will you?" I asked.

"Sorry, I'm going out to play ball," he replied. "Some friends and I have a game going."

"Mother!" I yelled. "Why don't you make Philip help?"

She appeared in the kitchen doorway, wiping her hands all over her dress. "Mind your own business, young lady!" she shouted. "Philip has a baseball game. I told him he could go."

"See you later," Philip called, shooting out the door.

"How come Philip can go play baseball, and I have to work?" I yelled. "You treat me like a slave."

"You have no respect, Denise, absolutely no respect!" Mom yelled back. "I told you I'm the one who gives the orders around here. Now get back to work!"

I didn't feel like arguing, so I went back to picking up the mess in the living room. I hated housework, but I realized that a certain amount of it was necessary.

I finally got through and turned on the TV again. Mom must have been listening for that moment, for she appeared in the doorway again, this time yelling, "Who told you that you could sit down?"

"Aw, Mom, I wanted to catch this program, and—"

The next thing I knew she had grabbed my arm and jerked me out of the chair. "You're not finished yet!" she announced.

"What do you mean?" I protested. "This room hasn't looked this good in ten years! Check it out!"

Without even bothering to look around she started dragging me to the kitchen, yelling, "There are still dirty dishes in the sink!"

"Hey, I cleaned the living room," I shouted, trying

desperately to grab onto something and pull away.
"Why don't you tell Dagmar to do the dishes? She hasn't
done any work today!"

By this time Mom had pulled me all the way across
the kitchen and stationed me in front of the sink. She
pointed at the sink filled with dirty dishes and ordered,
"Now get busy on those—and no complaining!"

When I looked, I realized that dirty dishes flowed beyond the sink onto all the counter tops. There were so
many dirty dishes that I was absolutely overwhelmed.

"Come on, Mom; give me a break, will you?" I
begged.

"Denise, I'm going to tell you something right to your
face," she said, pointing her index finger right at my
nose. "You've got a stubborn streak in you, and it's
going to have to be knocked out of you. Somehow, some
way you're going to have to learn to do what you're told.
Now get started on those dishes, and I don't want to hear
you open your mouth again!"

I glared at the monster. "Why are you picking on me
like this?" I demanded.

"I said not another word!" she replied. "So you can
add setting the table to your work."

She turned and stepped toward the stove. I almost
said something else but thought better of it. She'd find
work for me to do from now until kingdom come if I
didn't snap to.

I grabbed a heavy glass and looked over at her. Why,
I could throw it at her and hit her in the back of the
head! It would at least knock her out—maybe even put
her out of my life for good! I gritted my teeth and took
my time aiming. I'd probably only get one shot at this.

But just then Dagmar came prancing into the kitchen
and said, "Mom, is it okay if I go over to Becky's before
we eat? We've got to work on some algebra together."

When Mom said, "Sure, honey, that's okay," I nearly

exploded. She let Philip go play baseball; she let Dagmar go to a friend's house to study; she made me stay here and work. It just wasn't fair!

Dagmar hugged Mom and said, "I'll be back before six."

That's when I lost my temper. "What about me?" I yelled. "How come I can't go visit my friends? Why do I always have to be the slave around here?"

Mom spun around to confront me, a huge butcher knife still in her hand. She headed toward me, the knife raised.

"Mom, put that down!" Dagmar screamed. "Don't do something like that!"

I jumped behind Dagmar, knowing I'd be safe there, and pushed her toward Mom. This whole scene was unreal. I must be dreaming! What was happening to Mom? And why was she trying to kill me?

"Put down that knife!" Dagmar commanded.

I was surprised when Mom obeyed, even if it was reluctantly. Believe me, I began to breathe a little easier. Until you've gone through an experience like that, you have no idea what it's like to have your own mother threatening to kill you!

"What is going on around here?" Dagmar demanded.

"Your snotty little sister has been acting up lately," Mom explained lamely. "I've decided it's time for her to change her ways. And one of the ways she's going to have to change is to learn how to take care of a house. I may not be the best housekeeper in the world, but I think I can teach her a few things. Today she is learning to clean up the bathroom and her room, to tidy up the living room, and to do all those dirty dishes."

"Dagmar, how come Philip can go play baseball, you can go study with a friend, and I've got to stay here and work?" I wailed. "It just isn't fair."

I always looked up to Dagmar, and she treated me

well. In fact, she looked out for me, even lining me up with some boyfriends and double-dating with me.

"Yes, Mom, that's a good question," Dagmar said. "How come Denise has to do all the work? You're making this whole thing sound like Cinderella."

"You stay out of this, honey," Mom purred to Dagmar. "I know what I'm doing. Your sister really needs to change her ways. I don't expect her to like what I'm doing now, but someday she'll thank me for this."

I sputtered something, but Dagmar put her finger to her lips, signaling to me to be still. Then she grabbed the dishcloth, cleared some dishes out of the sink, and started the water. Once again Mom turned her back to us. At least she wasn't going to kill me now. And Dagmar was going to help me.

She even sang as she washed, trying to break the tension, I guess.

But I couldn't get the wild event out of my mind— Mom standing there with that knife poised, ready to strike me! Maybe this was a nightmare! It had to be.

As fast as Dagmar washed, I wiped and put the dishes in the cupboard. Nobody was talking. But I sure was thinking. Why did my mother continually make such a difference between the way she treated my brother and sister, and the way she treated me? It was almost as if she didn't love me as she did them. A real mother wouldn't try to kill her daughter, would she? Hey! Maybe that was it! Maybe she wasn't my real mother! That had to be it! I was adopted!

Every now and then I glanced over to where she stood over the stove, stirring whatever was in that pot for what seemed like the longest time.

When Dagmar and I finished the dishes and set the table, she asked, "Mom, is there anything else you'd like us to do?"

I was surprised when Mother didn't answer Dagmar.

She just kept stirring whatever it was she was cooking.

"Mom, what's the matter?" Dagmar asked.

Still silence.

Dagmar moved next to her, put her arm around Mom's shoulder, and asked again, "What's the matter?"

Then I noticed Mom's shoulders start to shake as she began to sob.

"Mom, what's wrong?" Dagmar pressed. "Why are you crying?"

I wanted to walk over and put my arms around her too. Dagmar could do that so easily. But I didn't think she'd want me to. In fact, I never could remember my mom hugging me.

"Mom, are we out of money again?" Dagmar asked.

Mom shook her head.

"Are you and Dad having problems again?"

"No, it's not that," she said between sobs.

"Tell me, Mom, what it is. Maybe Denise and I can help."

Suddenly Mom spun around and pushed Dagmar away and burst out of the kitchen, crying hysterically.

We could hear her sobbing upstairs in her bedroom. Something terrible must be wrong. But what? And how did I figure in all this? Somehow I suspected I was at the center of it.

"What in the world do you think is bothering her?" I asked Dagmar.

"I think—I—I—" Her voice trailed off, and I stood there waiting for her revelation. But then she turned and headed for the front door, grabbing her algebra book on the way. Dagmar apparently had some idea of what was wrong with Mother. But why wouldn't she tell me?

2

Since Dagmar had left without telling me what she thought was wrong with Mother, and since Mother wasn't about to tell me herself, I ambled back into the living room and plopped down in front of the TV. It was still blaring.

I had barely gotten involved in a show when I heard my mother lumbering down the stairs. This time without waiting for her to confront me, I hurried toward her and asked, "Mom, is there something else I can do to help?"

I noticed the muscles in her face tense. Then she snarled, "You just keep your big fat mouth shut, young lady. This is none of your business!"

She pushed by me into the kitchen. So help me, I never could figure her out. When I fussed about doing work, she was all over me. Then when I offered to help, she acted as if I had spit in her face! What was I supposed to do?

Well, I did what I usually did in a crisis. I went back to the living room to watch TV. It had become an escape from reality that I used more and more frequently.

But this time I couldn't concentrate on the program. I kept trying to figure out why my mother acted as she did toward me. Obviously she hated me, but she didn't hate Dagmar or Philip. Why? Could it be that I was adopted?

When Dad came home from work, he looked around in shock, and asked, "Denise, what on earth happened to our living room?"

"I cleaned it up," I announced proudly.

Coming over and sitting on the arm of my chair, Dad put his arms around me and hugged me tightly. "You'll make some lucky guy a good wife," he said. "I didn't know you were such a good housekeeper."

I wasn't too happy about Dad's analysis of man-woman relationships—that all I was good for was to be a good little housekeeper. But this wasn't the time to argue the point. Besides, every time my dad hugged me, it really made me feel loved. It was just as if I'd taken a good warm bath. His hugs seemed to be able to heal any hurt I had.

"Don't give me too many congratulations," I warned. "Mom was on her high horse and made me do all this."

Mom must have heard Dad come in, for she now appeared at the doorway whining, "Cecil, your snotty little daughter got smart with me today. I had to straighten her out."

"Oh, Mom, it wasn't that bad," I retorted. "At least I cleaned up this room and helped Dagmar with the dishes. Can't you give me credit for that much?"

With a loud, "Harrump!" she cleared her throat, spun around, and headed back into the kitchen.

"You don't love me!" I yelled.

It was as if the words turned her back my way again. She marched toward me, shouting, "Cecil, this daughter of yours is the worst kid in the world. If she were only like Philip or Dagmar, this would be a house of peace. But she's a monster, a real monster!"

"Now wait a minute!" Dad said. "What on earth is going on around here anyway?"

"Mom and I had some differences of opinion," I announced. "And in the process she yanked my hair, struck me, and even kicked me in the ribs. And I hadn't done one thing wrong!"

In an instant Mom was right in front of me, her fist drawn, ready to strike. Fortunately for me Dad grabbed her arm before she could cut loose. "For crying out loud!" he shouted, "this has got to stop! Here I come home from work, expecting a little peace and quiet, and I find myself right smack in the middle of a war! Now before you two start fighting again, I've got a little piece of news for you. I lost my job today."

"You did what?" Mom asked incredulously, turning toward him. "You lost your job?"

Dad nodded.

Mom looked at him with utter loathing and spit the words out, "Cecil, you're a good-for-nothing bum. You never could hold a job!"

"Come on now, Harriet," Dad protested weakly, "that's not true. I've been working hard. It wasn't because of my performance. Things are really slow down at the agency. That meant less work for the mechanics. You know I've told you that this was likely to happen, Harriet. Now quit blaming me. It's not my fault!"

Poor Dad. It would be bad enough to lose your job— but then to be accused of being a good-for-nothing bum! That thoughtless woman! Couldn't she see what she was doing to him?

"I'm sorry, Dad," I said, slipping my arm around him. "But you're a good mechanic. I'm sure something will turn up."

"Not around here," he replied. "There are too many mechanics out of work and looking. But my boss said he thought I might be able to find something at the Wing Airplane Company in Wichita, Kansas."

"An airplane company in Kansas?" I asked in surprise. "I thought you worked on cars."

"Well, it's like this," Dad said, sitting on the sofa and motioning to me to sit beside him. "My boss has a brother who works out there. He talked to him last night, and his brother said the company just got a good government contract, and they're hiring right now. He thought if I went out there with his brother's recommendation, I could probably get a job."

We were living in New Jersey, and Wichita, Kansas, seemed a world away.

I started to protest that I didn't want to leave all my high-school friends, when Mom plopped into a chair and said, "I assume you're planning to go alone?"

"I think that would be best," Dad replied. "If I get a job, then I'll come and get the rest of the family and move out there."

"Wichita, Albuquerque, Pocatello," Mom said. "It's all the same. Cecil, I just wish you'd settle down and get yourself a permanent job. Ever since I married you it's been this way. I never seem to have enough money for groceries. All day long I get calls about overdue bills. You'll never change. You're just a bum. You always think the grass is greener in the next pasture!"

"Harriet, button your lip, before I do it for you!" Dad shouted, jumping up and heading in her direction. "You stop talking like that!" Then he added, almost apologetically, "You know I've tried to do my best."

"Sure, you tried to do your best!" Mom responded sarcastically. "And we're living in poverty today because that's your best! You never could keep a steady job."

"That's not fair!" Dad exploded again. "Whenever

they lay me off, they always say it's not the quality of my work. And they say they'll be calling me back in a week or so. I can't help it if the weeks turn into months. I don't control the economy of this country!"

I couldn't believe how unfair and unfeeling my mother was being. Dad did try hard. He was a good man. He was always helping out someone who was having car trouble, and most of those people just said thanks—they never paid him for his time. And Dad was too proud to suggest it.

I'd noticed before how Mom seemed to take advantage of every opportunity to belittle Dad. It was hard to believe that long ago they might have really loved each other. There wasn't much evidence of it now.

I could tell Dad was raging. He turned on his heel and headed upstairs to change—and cool off. Mom, with great effort, pulled herself out of the chair and headed back to the kitchen. And once again I turned my attention to the TV, which had been adding its noise to all the commotion.

Right at six Philip returned from his ball game, happy as could be. And Dagmar came back smiling too. They were so good—so prompt, so obedient, so happy—that it disgusted me. Why was I such a misfit?

We all found our way to the kitchen for supper. And the silence around that table was unbearable. Even Dagmar and Philip sensed that Mom and Dad had been going at it.

Finally I couldn't stand it any longer and asked, "Why doesn't someone say something?"

"I won the ball game with a home run," Philip ventured.

"Mom told me Dad was going to Wichita to look for work," Dagmar said.

"Wichita?" Philip asked.

"Yes, but we don't have to go yet," Dagmar responded. "I guess this is kind of a good-bye supper for Dad. I think we should celebrate."

"That's it!" Mom shouted, slapping her hand on the table in delight. "We'll celebrate. Don't you children know that this good-for-nothing bum of a father of yours is going to go clear to Kansas? Maybe he'll get lost along the way and never come back!"

"Mother!" I protested.

"Harriet, that's enough of your nonsense!" Dad shouted, glaring daggers at her.

"My nonsense?" Mom shouted back. "Cecil, I think it's time the children knew what was going on around here!"

Dagmar's eyes were fixed on her plate. Apparently she knew what was coming next. I sure didn't.

"Children," Mom announced, "I think you should know that your dear father has been tomcatting around. He's got a girl friend on the side and is embarrassing me in front of this whole town!"

In an instant Dad pushed back his chair, jumped up from the table, banged his fist down, and yelled, "That's a dirty, filthy lie, Harriet! And you know it!"

"Cecil, don't call me names, and don't yell at me!" Mom shouted. "You think I don't know what's been going on? Every night when you leave here, I know where you're going—over to Beverly Olson's house!"

"That's no secret!" Dad shot back. "Of course I've been over there the last three nights. Hank was there too."

"You're the liar!" Mom shouted. "I called over there the other night, and she was the one who answered the phone. It was just you and Beverly over there!"

"Look, if you're going to play amateur detective, get your facts straight!" Dad yelled. "The reason she answered the phone was that Hank and I were outside in his garage overhauling the engine on that old Mercury he bought. It needed a ring job. And that's the truth!"

Mom grabbed her knife, pointed it in Dad's direction, and shouted, "That's a lie! That's a lie!"

Dad was so angry that he stomped out of the kitchen, his supper almost untouched. He headed for the front door, but before he left, he turned and shouted, "Children, don't believe her lies. She's sick. She's gone off her nut!"

I saw fire shooting from Mom's eyes as she retorted, "Your father's the one who's sick, children. Maybe it's a good thing he'll be away for a while."

With that she started wolfing down all the food in sight, including what Dad had left on his plate. She looked like a live version of Miss Piggy! Oh, it was disgusting!

By this time I'd lost my appetite. All I could think of was getting away from this terrible atmosphere for a while. So I excused myself, grabbed my coat, and headed into the cool evening air. It felt so invigorating that I decided to walk the few blocks to the pizza parlor nearby. I didn't have money for a pizza, but some of the kids from school hung out there. Maybe there would be somebody I could talk to—without getting hassled.

As I approached, I noticed Frank Burke standing by the door. He was still in school, although the word was around that he was there for the most part to push drugs. I wasn't into that kind of thing, so I didn't know for sure. But I usually avoided him.

I couldn't totally ignore him as I walked by him into the pizza place because he said, "Hi, Denise. How are you doing?"

When I stopped momentarily, he grabbed my arm. I tried to shake loose, saying, "I'm just fine, thank you."

I guess I was surprised that he let go of me so quickly. Maybe he was just trying to be polite. Maybe I was too hasty.

He followed me in and then asked, "Can I buy you a pizza?"

Figuring that maybe I'd been rude to him, and also that a pizza would indeed be tasty, I found myself saying, "Sure. Why not?"

I slipped into a booth as he went to the counter to order. Then he came back over and said, "I forgot to ask what you wanted on it, so I told him the works. Okay?"

"Great!" I responded.

And when the pizza came, I couldn't believe all the toppings. Oh, it looked luscious!

"What are you doing here so early in the evening?" he asked.

I sure didn't want to tell him about our family squabble. Besides, I had just taken a big bite of pizza before he asked, and there was no way I could answer.

"Come on, Denise," he said. "What's a nice girl like you doing here?"

"Eating pizza's no crime, is it?" I asked.

"You know what I mean," he said. "This place doesn't have exactly the best reputation in town."

"Yeah, but it's got good pizza!" I said. "I've been here several times. My folks brought me here once. It's the closest pizza place to where we live."

Frank smiled benignly and said, "You're stupid, man; really stupid!"

I put down the piece of pizza and pushed back a little bit. I didn't like anybody calling me names—not my mother, not my dad, not my sister, not my brother, and certainly not this little two-bit drug pusher!

So I said, "Please don't call me stupid, Frank. I resent that. I deeply resent that."

He laughed easily. "You sure have a low boiling point, don't you?"

Chagrined, I nodded.

"Look, baby, I wasn't trying to make you mad," he

said, reaching across and touching my arm gently. "I was just trying to tell you something."

"Like what?"

"Don't you know that outside this place is where everybody deals in drugs?"

"Of course I know that. Everybody knows that."

I really didn't know it, but I sure wasn't going to admit that Frank was right in calling me stupid.

"When I saw you walking up," Frank went on, "I figured you'd come to buy some pot. And, confidentially, I've got some good pot."

I knew it! He was trying to get me hooked on drugs!

"Well, Frank, thanks for the offer, but no thanks," I replied. "I'm not into that."

"Hey, everybody says that until they try it," he replied, stuffing half of a slice of pizza into his mouth. "But, baby, pot is the answer to everything you've ever wanted! Every problem will just dissolve as soon as you inhale the stuff."

I licked some cheese off my finger and said, "Frank, if you think that buying me a pizza is going to make me a customer for your drugs, you've got another thing coming. Now take your pizza and stuff it up your nose!"

With that outburst I pushed my way out of the booth and headed for the exit. In an instant Frank jumped up and grabbed my shoulder. "Sit down, will you?" he said. "You're a nice girl. I know that. I would never sell you any pot, and I'd beat up any pusher who tried to sell it to you. And if you asked me to sell you some, I'd tell you what you could do with your money. No way am I going to ruin a good girl like you! Baby, I've had my eye on you at school, and I like what I see. And I like it the way I see it now. Do I make myself clear?"

That sounded more like it. Besides, I was a little flattered that he had noticed me. So I slowly sat down again, and, smiling, Frank pushed the pizza toward me.

I grabbed another yummy slice and savored all those flavors. . . .

Frank leaned across the table and asked, "Want a Coke?"

I spit out the pizza and protested, "Frank, for crying out loud, I told you I don't do drugs—no pot, no coke, nothing!"

He hee-hawed. "I mean Coca-Cola," he told me. "Denise, I wish you wouldn't be so uptight."

How embarrassing! I knew coke was the street name for cocaine and was trying to show off my knowledge.

"What I mean is, how about a Pepsi, or a 7-Up, or a root beer?" Frank said. "Or do you want milk?"

I giggled. "Coke will be fine," I responded.

The way Frank smiled at me made butterflies flutter in the pit of my stomach. I'd always thought of him as a sleazy character, but I was seeing a side of him now that I'd never seen before. Actually, he was kind of attractive, strangely attractive, in a different sort of way.

When he brought the soft drink, he bowed slightly and said, "Madam, here is your Coke. Do you want to sniff it?"

"A straw will do just fine," I said, giggling again.

"Hey, that's better!" Frank said, patting my hand. "I like you when you loosen up a little. You're an okay kid. But I get the distinct feeling that something's really bothering you tonight. What is it?"

"No problem," I lied. "I just got my report card with all *A*s on it, and so I'm here to celebrate."

"Don't tell me I'm sharing pizza with an intellectual!" Frank said in surprise. "That'll ruin my image!"

"No, just kidding. It's my sis who makes the good grades," I said. "It was just that I needed to get out of the house for a while tonight. That's why I came here."

"Hey, I know what that's all about, man," Frank said, leaning back and laughing. "I need to get out of the house all the time. My old man and old lady are always on the warpath—always drunk. It's hell at my house."

I don't know why I said it. Maybe I felt that Frank would understand. But I blurted out, "Yeah, but I bet your old lady doesn't beat up on you like mine does on me!"

Frank leaned forward and confided, "They're both always beating on me. Here. Let me show you something."

He pulled up his shirt, and I spotted the terrible black-and-blue marks on his ribs. "Two cracked ribs," he announced. "My old man took a baseball bat to me when he was drunk a couple of weeks ago."

"Frank, I bet you got that in a fight," I said.

Frank wasn't grinning now as he tucked his shirt back in. "I'm not kidding, Denise. That's why I spend so much time out on the streets. My parents are sick."

"Well, why don't you do something about it?" I asked, trying to be sympathetic.

"Are you kidding? What can I do? Call the cops?"

"Yeah. Call the cops. Child abuse is against the law."

"Denise, I called you stupid a little while ago," Frank said. "I was kidding then. Now I'm about ready to mean it."

"What are you talking about?"

"Well, I've been busted three times by the cops for stealing. Now I don't want you to feel sorry for me, and I'm not making excuses for stealing. But we don't have a single thing at our house. I mean, not one thing. A couple of years ago I used to walk by this place and envy all the people sitting inside eating pizza and laughing and giggling and having a good time. I couldn't come in. I had no money. So one night I decided to steal some things so I could get some money and buy pizza like everybody else. I got my pizza all right, but the cops soon came looking for me."

I wasn't sure why Frank was telling me all this, but he really had my attention now.

"I guess I was kind of lucky," Frank went on. "The cops told me not to do it again. Well, I did it again. And again. So far I've stayed out of the slammer. But if I call the cops on my old man and old lady, with my record, do you think for a minute those cops are going to listen to me?"

I stared in disbelief. I had no idea Frank's homelife was like this.

"Well, I never stole to get a pizza," I said. "I was lucky enough to have a nice young man offer to buy me one."

He smiled.

"And although my old lady hates me and knocks me around," I went on, "my dad loves me."

"I wish I could say that," Frank said thoughtfully. Maybe I could take it if one of them loved me. But both of them are crazy out of their heads."

"Frank, we have something in common," I said. I lifted my sweater a little and pointed: "That's where my old lady kicked me this afternoon."

"Hey, we're twins!" Frank exclaimed, moving over next to me and gently touching my side.

"Ouch! That hurts!" I yelled, pulling away.

"You'd better believe it hurts!" Frank replied. "I know exactly how you feel!"

Then he began rubbing his fingers gently on my ribs. He was getting a little too personal, but it did feel good.

"Does it hurt up here?" he asked.

His fingers were up too high. I looked into his eyes and protested, "You fresh thing!"

Frank quickly pulled his hand away. "I just couldn't help it," he said. "You set yourself up."

We both laughed easily. Somehow I felt he understood what I was going through. Both of us had family problems. Both of us had been hit in the ribs by angry parents.

Easing a little closer, Frank said, "Denise, I know a way to get rid of all those problems you're having. I mean, *all* of them."

Was there really an answer, a way to get rid of all your troubles? I knew there wasn't. But I kept hoping that maybe a fairy godmother would wave a magic wand over me.

"You know how to solve those problems?" Frank asked gently.

"Sure," I replied. "You knock off both parents."

Frank smiled. "That's the hard way," he said. "Man, I know the easy way out."

"Frank, there is no easy way out," I replied.

He smiled and said, "Trust me." Was he about to give me the answer to all my problems? I should have known that he really couldn't. But his invitation was so inviting. . . .

3

As I finished the last slice of pizza, Frank grabbed my arm and exclaimed, "Come on! Let's go!"

"Where?" I asked as I came flying along behind him.

"It's not far," he reassured me. "We are going to happy land."

"Happy land?" I repeated in surprise. "Come on, Frank; don't give me any nonsense. Tell me where we're headed."

"Just a couple of blocks," he answered, still pulling me along.

He seemed so strong, so sure of himself, that I found it easy to go wherever he was leading.

But when we started down an alley, I began to get a little edgy. I guess Frank realized that because he gently took my arm and assured me everything was going to be all right. Somehow I felt safer.

About halfway down the alley, we came to a doorway.

When Frank opened the door and stood back for me to enter, I protested, "No way, Frank!"

"Denise, please don't act that way," he pleaded. "This is all okay. Nothing bad will happen to you. Now trust me."

"Frank, I—I—I think I'd better go home," I stammered. "I've been gone too long now. My mother will be worried."

"From what you've told me about her, I doubt that!" Frank countered. "Now just give me five minutes. Okay? Just five minutes."

I worried about what he had in mind. He didn't think I'd go to bed with him, did he? I sure wasn't that kind of girl.

I started edging away from the door. Frank caught my arm and said, "Please don't be afraid. All I want you to do is meet a friend of mine."

A friend? Well, this should be all right then if someone else was around.

We walked up the stairs, down a hallway, and to an apartment door which Frank opened. A blast of music greeted us.

Over on the sofa sat a man of rather slight build. His thinning hair made him look to be in his forties. I didn't remember ever seeing him around town.

When he saw me, he jumped up and demanded, "What's that broad doing here?"

"Hey, Mr. Galogan, no problem, no problem!" Frank responded. "She's a friend of mine."

The man pointed toward the door we had just entered and screamed, "Get her out of here right now! I won't have any broads coming up here with you!"

Frank bristled and responded, "Hey, wait just a minute! I thought any friend of mine would be a friend of yours. This girl's okay, man; she's okay."

"You heard me, Frank. Get her out of here right now!"

I had no earthly idea of what was going on, but when that angry-looking man started toward me, I decided it would be foolish to wait around and find out. I headed for the door and heard footsteps right behind me.

I didn't stop until I was back down in the alley and realized it was Frank who had followed me out. Frank's friend had apparently stayed in the apartment.

"What was that all about?" I asked. "I mean, that guy must be off the wall!"

"Please don't talk that way," Frank told me. "After all, Mr. Galogan did take me in."

"Take you in?" I asked in surprise. "How long have you been staying with him, Frank?"

"A week yesterday. I didn't have a place to go. I met Mr. Galogan on the street; we got to talking, and he offered to let me stay in his apartment for a while."

"How much do you know about him?" I asked.

"Not much. He's new here in town."

"Frank," I said, measuring my words, "I don't want to alarm you, and I may be wrong, but that guy looks like a homosexual to me. Surely you've been reading in the papers about the rash of teenage boys being murdered by perverted homosexuals, haven't you?"

He looked at me in surprise.

"Do you know anything about him?" I repeated.

"Just as I said. I was out in the street. My old man and old lady said that now that I was eighteen, I needed to learn to make my own way and not be a drag on them. I mean, they threw me out! Well, I met Mr. Galogan. True, I'd never seen him before, but he seemed like a decent enough man. I had no place to go, so when he invited me to live with him, it just seemed like the thing to do."

"Frank, I don't mean to get nosy or anything, and you

can tell me it's none of my business if you want to, but
has that guy tried anything? I mean, when I mentioned
the possibility that he might be gay, you looked pretty
shocked, as though that idea hadn't occurred to you
before."

Frank stared at the ground.

"Listen, Frank," I said, pulling his face up to make
him look at me. "I'm not here to tell you what you
should or should not be doing. But I'm worried about
you. This guy may be up to no good. I mean, he may be
perverted. He could kill you!"

Frank deliberately turned away from me.

"Frank," I insisted, "are you involved with that guy?"

He finally turned toward me, a look of pleading in his
eyes. "Listen, Denise, you've got to believe me. The guy
made some advances. But I acted as though I didn't
have any idea of what he had in mind. I swear I haven't
done a thing. But what was I going to do when my folks
threw me out? Sleep on the streets?"

"Frank, there are worse things than sleeping in the
streets."

"You really think I'm in danger?" he asked nervously.

"Are you kidding?" I responded. "Of course, I can't
be positive, but all the signs point that way. Look how
possessive he has become of you. He doesn't even want
you to have a friend who is a girl."

"But he was nice to me," Frank said, apparently un-
willing to admit the obvious. "He took me in when I had
no place to go. He cooks delicious meals for me. He
gives me money. I'm a little worried, but I have no other
place to go."

"But, Frank, the guy's a homosexual. You admitted
he's made advances. It isn't going to be long before
you're going to be forced to pay him back for those
meals and the place to stay. Do you know what I mean?"

"I know; I know!" Frank responded. "But what am I going to do?"

I grabbed his arm and started pulling him toward the street. "I know what you're going to do," I announced. "You're going to go home with me!"

"Really? Do you really mean it?"

"Well, we can try it. But for crying out loud, get out of that apartment. I think there's real danger there."

We both turned when we heard footsteps behind us, running toward us. Then Mr. Galogan shouted, "Young lady, you get out of here and leave Frank alone, or I'm going to have to call the cops."

Frank was obviously torn between going with me and staying with Mr. Galogan. I started backing away, but Frank stood transfixed on the spot. Then I heard Mr. Galogan say sweetly, "Frank, come on home. I've got an apple pie baked and some ice cream I fixed for you. But that tramp you're with—she's not walking into my place!"

He stared at me icily, venting all the hatred he felt toward women.

"I'm leaving, Frank," I announced. "You can come with me if you want to."

I backed toward the street, keeping an eye on the man. There was no telling what he might do to keep Frank. He might even pull a gun and shoot me, telling Frank he was doing him a favor to get rid of me!

Frank spoke hesitatingly. "Mr. Galogan, I think . . . I think I'm going with Denise. She's—"

"Oh, no you're not!" Mr. Galogan shrieked, leaping toward Frank. "You're mine! You're mine!"

I took off as fast as I could go, and Frank was right alongside me, with Mr. Galogan running after us, cursing me and pleading with Frank.

We took a right as we got to the street, and then I noticed that the shouts and curses were getting softer.

Looking back, I realized that Mr. Galogan had stopped at the street. But he was waving his fist at us and still shouting.

Frank and I ran several more blocks until we just dropped to the curb, exhausted.

"I can't believe how close that was," I told Frank. "That guy wanted to possess you. Did you hear him hollering, 'You're mine'? You were lucky to get away!"

"I know you're right, Denise. All along I knew I was heading for trouble. But I never could get up the courage to break away from the guy. It was almost as if he had some sort of a spell over me."

We sat there holding hands and catching our breath. Then we started in the direction of my house.

"Denise, I'm sorry for the way I've messed up your evening," Frank said apologetically. I don't know when I've ever been so scared."

"Me too!" I announced. "That creep looked as though he could have done me in without any pangs of conscience!"

"I've got something that will take away all those fears," Frank announced, reaching into his pocket. There I was looking at two sticks of pot.

"Frank, come on," I protested. "I told you I don't want to smoke that stuff. I'm no junkie."

"Hey, hey," Frank replied, laughing. "I'm no junkie either. But I've discovered that just a little pot takes away all your fears. And I need something to take away my fears right now!"

He lit up and inhaled deeply. His face suddenly looked so peaceful, that when he held the stick out to me, I grabbed it. Everything in me said not to do it. But I did it anyway. Maybe it was because I really was scared. Maybe I was upset by what had happened in my family. Maybe it was because I really wanted to do something to please Frank. I wanted him to like me and hated for him to think of me as a prude.

The next thing I knew I was inhaling deeply, just as he told me to do. Then I felt it—a little tingling sensation coming from deep within and spreading throughout my body.

Frank took the joint from my hand and took another drag. Then I took it from him, and we kept trading back and forth until it was gone. Then he lit another one.

By the time we had finished the second stick, we were both giggling. Frank was right. I did feel calm and peaceful. Maybe pot was the answer to all my problems.

We were still laughing as we walked up to my house. At that point I didn't care what my parents said. If they threw him out, then I was going with him. I really felt good about Frank, about myself, about life. I was high, and this had to be the answer!

When we walked in the front door, the only person visible was my mother, and she was watching TV.

"Mom, this is a friend of mine, Frank Burke," I said.

She looked up momentarily at Frank, grunted something unintelligible, and turned back to watch TV. I wanted to grab her and shake her for being so rude to my friend.

Dad was sitting in the kitchen, having a cup of coffee, so I took Frank out there and introduced him.

Dad looked up, but he didn't smile or even offer his hand. He just said, "So you're the Burke boy, are you? I've met your parents a couple of times."

That was strange. Why would Dad know them?

"Dad, can Frank stay here tonight?" I asked.

His mouth flew open as he repeated, "Stay here tonight? I think Frank should go home to his parents, don't you?"

I didn't want to have to explain about his being thrown out of his home, so I said, "Well, it's just for tonight. I think he could probably go home tomorrow. Okay?"

Dad mumbled something and then said, "Denise, I need to talk to you about something for a minute. Come with me."

He led me down the hallway and upstairs, into my bedroom, and shut the door. Before I could say anything, he started in: "Denise, I don't know what I'm going to do with you. It was bad enough when you used to bring home stray puppies and kittens when you were little. But why did you bring that filthy bum here?"

"Dad, don't talk that way about Frank. If you only knew what he was up against, you wouldn't say things like that."

"Denise, I'm telling you, that young man is nothing but trouble! Don't you know he's been in trouble with the law? He's been busted for stealing, and he's been known to sell drugs around town. I want you to stay as far from him as you can!"

I was really ticked off at my dad, ready to judge Frank guilty without hearing the evidence. So I yelled, "Let me tell you what I know about Frank. His old man and old lady threw him out of his house. Without a place to go, he started wandering the streets and met this guy who invited him to his apartment. Frank's been living there for a week. I just came from that apartment, and we barely escaped with our lives!"

"What?" Dad asked, startled. "You did what?"

"Frank ended up staying with a homosexual. The guy went absolutely off his rocker when Frank brought me up to introduce me to him. I mean, he is really trying to dominate Frank. The whole thing is really suspicious. Frank said he hasn't done anything with the guy, but he is worried. Dad, you've read about those homosexual murders, haven't you? Well, this looks like another one of those situations. I grabbed Frank, and we ran away from that creep. I think he would have killed me if he

had caught me. Anyway, that's what happened and why
I brought Frank here. He needs a place to spend the
night."

"Denise, are you making this up?"

"Dad, every word is the truth. When you left the table
all upset tonight, I lost my appetite over the way Mother
was treating you. I needed some fresh air and went for a
walk. When I walked by the pizza place, Frank and I got
to talking. He invited me to his apartment to meet his
friend. I didn't know I was going to meet a weirdo. I tell
you, Dad, something is drastically wrong with that
whole situation. I think I rescued Frank from certain
death!"

"But, Denise, we can't have Frank staying here, especially with my going away tomorrow. I believe what you
told me, but I also believe some of the other things I've
heard about that boy. I've gotten information from some
pretty reliable sources. Taking on a delinquent boy is
not like training a puppy, Denise. No way are you going
to change that boy. Instead you'll end up being like
him."

If Dad knew I had just smoked pot with Frank, he'd
have the clincher for his argument and would probably
forbid me ever to see him again.

So I said, "Dad, you're probably right. You usually
are. Go ahead and throw him out. But you might as well
get ready to throw me out too. And when you throw me
out, what's going to happen to me? I mean, if I have no
place to go, where will I end up? What happens to those
girls who get thrown out of their homes and end up in
New York City?"

I waited.

"You know what happens, Dad. Pimps get them.
They become junkies. They become prostitutes. Why?
Because their parents had no understanding of their
problems and threw them out!"

The more I talked, the madder I got. But I could tell
Dad was getting my point.

"Come on, Denise, be fair," he replied. "You can't
blame it all on the parents. It's the kids who make the
choices."

"Maybe so, but it's still the parents who throw them
out! But let's get back to Frank. That weirdo he was living with had made some advances. It wouldn't be long
before Frank would be doing things he never thought
he'd be doing. And why would that happen?"

I waited for it to sink in, but Dad just shrugged.

"Dad!" I yelled. "Poor Frank is going to be the slave
to that man's lust because his parents threw him out of
the house. None of this would even have started if they
hadn't told Frank to leave."

Dad had turned away from me, and I grabbed him
and wheeled him around to face me. "Dad, if you throw
Frank out of our house tonight, the poor boy has only
one place to go—back to that weirdo. And when Frank
comes up missing in a few weeks, I'm going to hold you
personally responsible for his murder. Do you know
what some of those perverted weirdos do to teenage boys
like Frank?"

After a long pause Dad said lamely, "Okay, you've
made your point. I don't like the idea, but he can stay
here tonight—and tonight only. I leave for Wichita tomorrow, and there's absolutely no way that boy can stay
here after that. You'll have to figure out something
tomorrow."

I walked back downstairs beaming. I had done it!

Frank wasn't in the kitchen where I had left him. I
found him in the living room, talking to my mother.
When she saw me, she said, "Denise, where have you
been hiding this wonderful boy? He's so interesting."

"I really enjoyed getting acquainted with your mom,"
Frank told me. "She's a great gal."

I couldn't believe it! Frank already had my mom wrapped around his little finger. Talk about a charmer!

Dad had followed me down the stairs and announced, "Harriet, Frank doesn't have anywhere to stay tonight, so I told Denise he could stay with us for one night. Okay?"

Mom slapped her hands together and said excitedly, "That's great! I really want to get to know Frank better."

"Harriet, would you come upstairs and help me pack?" Dad asked.

I knew it was a ploy. Dad wanted to get her upstairs so he could fill her in on all the dirt he had on Frank. So I said, "Thanks, Dad, for that conversation we had. It's just between you and me. Right?"

I waited almost breathlessly for his answer. I sure didn't want him telling Mother what he had told me. I knew parts of it were true, although I'd never admit that to Dad. Finally Dad said, "Yes, darling, that conversation was just between you and me."

When my parents were gone, I snuggled up next to Frank and said in amazement, "How in the world did you get Mother on your side?"

He looked really pleased with himself and said, "It works every time."

"What works every time?"

"Listen, Denise, all you have to do is to tell people a really sad story. You don't have to lie, but give it all you've got. I told your mom how my parents were vicious and mean and drunkards and every bad thing I could think of. I told her how I'd been neglected and rejected—laying it on thick. Then I said how fortunate you and Dagmar were to be living in a house like this with a wonderful mother who seemed so full of love and compassion, raising such a wonderful family. She was practically eating out of my hand." He laughed again.

"You mean you set up my mother that obviously and she fell for it?"

"Denise, you've got to learn about human nature," Frank chided. "When you start to flatter people and build up their egos, they'll fall for anything! Flattery really gets them. And I pour it on, baby!"

I laughed, and he put his arm around me and gave me a little squeeze. This Frank was something else!

"Have you got any more pot?" I whispered.

"Sure do."

"Let's walk out back," I suggested.

We went out back into the garage and lit up in the darkness. We had almost finished the joint when suddenly the lights went on. I yanked the stick out of my mouth and threw it on the floor. But not in time, for there stood my mother!

"What on earth is going on out here?" she demanded.

I stuttered, trying to think of something to say. But Frank piped up with, "We're smoking pot."

That stupid Frank! I thought he was so smart, so cool. Why did he admit it? This was going to be nothing but trouble for me—and him too!

"Smoking pot?" Mom asked. "Where did you get it?"

"Well, I just happened to have a few joints with me, Mrs. Brady. Do you want some?"

I couldn't believe what I was hearing. No way would Frank be able to spend the night at our house now. He'd be lucky if Mom just threw him out and didn't call the cops!

"I've got another joint, Mrs. Brady," Frank said. "Denise and I were just going to smoke it. Why don't you join us?"

Mom hesitated and looked around to see if anyone else was there. Then she smiled faintly and said, "You know, I've always wondered about marijuana. I've heard some good things about it and lots of bad. But I've always had a secret desire to try it."

That was all the encouragement Frank needed. He quickly lit the stick, handed it to her and said, "Inhale, taking a deep breath. Then hold it."

When she did, it absolutely disgusted me—that big, fat slob, smoking pot! So when Frank took the stick and handed it to me, I pushed it away with, "No thanks, Frank. I'll see you later."

When I got back in the house, Dad was in the kitchen again. "Where'd your mother disappear to this time?" he asked.

What should I say? Should I lie and say I didn't know? Or should I shout that she was out in the garage with my boyfriend, smoking pot?

I decided that neither answer would work, so I just pushed by him into the living room and plopped down in front of the TV.

Dad followed me in, yelling, "I asked you a simple question. Where is your mother?"

How could I ever tell him?

4

There was Dad standing between me and the TV, waiting for my answer. I just couldn't tell him Mom was out in the garage, smoking pot with Frank.

"I noticed you just came in from the garage," Dad said. "Is your mother out in the garage?"

Thinking quickly I responded, "Yeah, she's out there with Frank. And you'd never believe what he said to her, Dad."

"What do you mean by that?"

"He is really straightening her out, Dad. I mean, you wouldn't believe what he is telling her—and she's listening! I believe that boy is going to help her!"

"Help her? That woman is beyond help."

"Dad, you would think that Frank had already raised ten kids. He is telling her how love and understanding go a lot further than hate, that hugging your children every morning does more than swearing at them. Honest, Dad, you wouldn't believe what is happening out there!"

At least my last sentence was correct! I studied Dad's features to see if my story was convincing.

Dad started pacing as he said, "Denise, I've been nervous ever since you brought that boy home. I know about him, and he's up to no good."

"Please, Dad, don't say that. I've gotten to know him a little, and he's not all bad. He's had some tough breaks and had to watch out for himself. But that's not his fault. Let him stay tonight, and we'll make other arrangements tomorrow. Okay?"

"Well, I don't think we can go that far with him."

"What do you mean by that?" I asked, jumping to my feet.

"Well, don't get mad at me, but I called the police to double-check on him, to see if those stories I've been hearing were correct."

"You called the police?" I echoed in shock. "Dad, Frank hasn't done anything."

"I didn't tell them he had," he replied edgily. "I just called to verify the information I had."

"Why, Dad?"

"Because, as I told you, I've been nervous about him ever since he came. He's known to the police as a no-good. His parents are deadbeats. I had to know about him."

What had Dad found out? Did he suspect we had been smoking pot? What would he say if he knew Mom was smoking it now?

"Denise, we've got a little problem," Dad went on.

"Dad, I'm really surprised at what you did," I said. "Just because Frank isn't lily white and has made a few mistakes, that doesn't give you the right to call the police to check on him."

"Well, it turns out that maybe I did the right thing,"

Dad replied smugly. "It seems that your Frank is in deep trouble."

Dad must know about the pot! I'd better cover for Frank.

"Well," I said, "whatever the police told you, I wouldn't believe them. They're always picking on poor kids, and they let the politicians' kids get by with murder. You know that's true."

"Denise, I don't know that's true. And it's beside the point. The police want to talk to Frank. They told me there's been a burglary this evening, and it's just like the others Frank pulled. When they found out Frank was here, they said they were looking for him and wanted to talk to him. The cops are on their way over here now."

"What?" I asked in shock. "Did I hear you right? Did you actually turn poor homeless Frank in to the cops? Dad, I—"

"Denise, I ought to knock some sense into your head," Dad interrupted. "There was a break-in at Rymers' place tonight. The cop told me that whenever there's any kind of a break-in, the first person they pick up for questioning is Frank. He's been busted before, you know. I told you that."

All the while we were talking I was trying to think of some way to warn Frank so he could take off before the cops arrived. And I was beginning to fit some things together about Frank. This was where he got his money for pot—by stealing. He had told me he stole, but I only half believed him. I thought maybe he was just bragging to try to impress me.

"The police assured me that all they wanted to do was ask Frank a few questions," Dad said lamely.

"Sure, Dad," I answered sarcastically. "Have you ever known a cop to say anything but that? They come out and ask a few questions, and then they say, 'We'll have to take you down to the station.' The next thing we know they'll have him in jail—and without any proof whatever. The cops just have it in for Frank. The poor guy doesn't have a chance. I'm not going to stand for this, Dad. I'm going out there and warn him so he can take off!"

Before I could get by him, Dad had grabbed my arm and shouted, "Now wait a minute! There are some real problems in this house. Your mom needs psychiatric help. I'm leaving tomorrow for Wichita to try to find work. And now we've got a gangster staying with us. I've got to have all these problems solved before I leave tomorrow. And nothing is going to happen to Frank if he's innocent."

I tried to jerk away from Dad's grip, but he pushed me into a chair and shouted, "Now you just sit there and behave yourself!"

"When was the Rymers' place knocked off?" I asked.

"The officer didn't say."

"Well, Dad, I've been with Frank since early this evening. I'm going to cover for him."

"Now listen here, Denise!" he shouted, his face getting redder. "This is serious. Our town has been plagued with burglaries. We've got to support the police. If Frank's the culprit, we have no right to keep him here. He needs to be put away."

Just then I heard the back door open and two voices giggling. I knew Frank and Mom were high.

When Mom saw Dad, she threw her arms around him and said, "Darling, this Frank Burke is a wonderful boy. I think we ought to keep him around here. He could protect us while you're in Wichita."

Dad started backing up. Did he suspect what she'd been doing? How much did he know about how people high on pot acted?

Next Mom turned her full attention to me, throwing her arms around me and hugging me. Any other time I would have been delighted if she hugged me. Now I felt nothing but loathing toward her.

Frank stood there smiling at his personal triumph. If he only knew what was about to happen.

When someone knocked at our door at that moment, I realized I had waited too long to tell Frank. Dad walked over and stood by Frank and said, "Denise, please answer the door."

I started toward the back door instead and said softly, "Frank, come here quick."

"Shall we talk in the garage?" Frank giggled.

"Frank, come now!" I ordered.

When he started toward me, Dad grabbed his arm, saying, "Now everybody remain calm. Denise, go open that door, as I told you."

Frank looked at my dad in surprise and asked, "What in the world is going on?"

"It's the cops, Frank!" I screamed. "It's the cops!"

Frank tried to jerk away, but Dad gripped tighter. They then tumbled to the floor.

The front door flew open, and there stood two cops, their guns drawn.

"Help me!" Dad yelled. "Help me!"

One of the cops was already there, grabbed his handcuffs, and slapped them on Frank. Then he jerked him to his feet.

Frank was cursing as Dad slowly got up. Suddenly I felt the same kind of loathing for Dad as I did for Mom. I just couldn't believe Dad would rat on somebody like this.

The cop had backed Frank against the wall and was warning him, "Young man, just settle down. Nobody is going to get hurt."

"You turkeys don't have a thing on me!" Frank yelled. "I haven't done anything wrong!"

"Nobody said you did," one of the cops responded.

"Now why don't we start by your telling us where you were this evening?"

"He's been with me!" I yelled. "And I know he's done nothing wrong."

"Where were you between seven and eight?" the cop asked Frank, ignoring me.

"I already told you he was with me!" I yelled again.

The officer looked my way and said, "Okay, where were the two of you at that time?"

"We were down at the pizza place on the highway," I said. "The owner can verify that. Then we went to the apartment of a friend of Frank. And we were back here before nine-thirty. Isn't that right, Mom?"

Mom nodded. "That's right, officers. I'm sure my daughter would tell the truth. Frank has been with my daughter, and he's been here at our house for quite some time now."

"Are you both telling me the truth?" the cop demanded.

I nodded, and so did Mom.

"Well, we'll have to take Frank in for questioning," the officer said. "It's routine. The Rymers think they got a look at the guy who broke in. We need to check this out."

With that they grabbed Frank and started pushing him toward the front door. I was furious at my dad for doing this. But I wanted Frank to know that as far as I was concerned, nothing had changed between us. So I called after him, "It's okay, Frank. I know everything's going to work out."

I was saying the right words, but I really wasn't believing them. How had I managed, in such a few short hours, to get myself into a mess like this? Was I trying to defend somebody who was guilty of a crime? Had Frank really broken into that house before I met him at the pizza place?

I was watching the cops push Frank into their patrol car when my dad pulled me inside the house and slammed the door. He glared at Mom and muttered, "Good riddance to bad rubbish!"

"Cecil, you're a beast!" Mom shouted. "How could you do that to that poor, innocent little boy? You are a beast!"

Whap! Dad backhanded her a hard one across the face, yelling, "Harriet, I know what I'm doing. I'm still in charge of this house!"

Mom let Dad have one across the face, and then the whole thing turned into a slapping war. "Stop it! Stop it!" I screamed.

It was like trying to talk to the wind. They were boiling mad at each other, and nothing was about to stop them. I didn't know which one I hated the most—Mom for the way she treated me, or Dad for calling the cops on Frank. And I was still mad at Mom for coming out there to the garage and taking Frank's attention away from me. Then I thought of a way I could get back at her. So I yelled, "Dad, you were right. That Frank is no good!"

They both stopped with their hands in midair and stared at me. Now I had them!

"Do you know what Mom was really doing out in the garage with Frank?" I said. "You wouldn't believe it!"

"Denise, you keep your fat mouth shut," Mom threatened, "or I'll shut it for you permanently!"

Dad grabbed both her arms and held her back as he said, "And what was she really doing out there in that garage?"

"She was smoking pot, Dad. She and Frank were smoking pot! Didn't you notice they were high when they came in?"

"What?" Dad yelled. "Harriet, were you out there smoking pot?"

Realizing she was in a corner, Mom just smiled, relaxed, and said, "Cecil, it felt so good."

Now what was Dad going to do?

He pushed her away, spun on his heel, and headed upstairs, shouting, "I've had enough of this crazy, cockeyed family for one night. I'm going to bed!"

Mom immediately started toward me, and I yelled, "Dad! Dad! She's going to beat me! Come quick!"

I headed for the stairs, knowing she was right behind me. Then I felt her grab my hair. I yelled again for Dad. He didn't even turn around.

Mom twisted my hair to spin me around, and then let me have it right across the face with her fist. As I was reeling from that blow, she kicked me in the stomach. The pain was excruciating!

My hands instinctively went to try to cover my stomach, and she slammed me in the face again. As I tried to protect my face, once again she kicked my stomach. I doubled over, and started falling. . . .

When I came to, the house was quiet. How long had I been out? Was everybody else asleep?

I heard a strange noise and realized someone was scratching at the window. I moved cautiously and then heard a voice whisper, "Denise, it's me."

I hurried outside and into Frank's arms. "Are you okay?" I asked. "Did you beat the rap?"

"Yeah, I didn't do the Rymers' place. They couldn't prove a thing, so they let me go."

"What are you going to do now?" I asked.

"Well, once again I'm trying to find a place to spend the night. Did you get things ironed out with your dad?"

"No, Frank. He's on the warpath about you. If he finds you here, he'll call the cops and make up some kind of story about you. Besides, I told him you and Mom were out in the garage smoking pot."

"You did what?"

"I told him what you were doing out there."

"Denise, that was stupid."

"Well, you told Mom what we were doing. Why shouldn't I tell Dad what you were doing? Besides, I don't like her pushing in when the two of us are around."

"Do I detect a little jealousy?" he teased.

"Well, all I know is that my old lady is a witch," I said, "and it was the only way I could think of to get even with her."

"I know what you mean," Frank sympathized. "I'd hate to have to live with the old bag. But she sure is easy to turn on!" He laughed heartily.

"Ssshh!" I cautioned. "Somebody will hear you. You stay here, and I'll get a few things together and we'll run away. Okay?"

"Denise, that wouldn't be wise," Frank said. "We need to think this through a little tomorrow. Why can't I just stay here tonight?"

"Frank, Dad would kill you!" I replied. "But maybe—Yeah! That's it! You can sleep in the garage. There's an old sleeping bag that Dad uses sometimes when he goes fishing. It's on a shelf out there. I'll bring out a couple of blankets. You'll have a roof over your head anyway."

"Hey, that sounds great!" Frank enthused. "Anything will be great if I'm close to you. But what about your dad?"

He's leaving early tomorrow for Wichita. He'll be taking that old car that's parked on the street. When he leaves, all you have to do is turn my old lady on, and she'll probably let you sleep in my dad's bed!"

Frank laughed. "I'd rather sleep in yours," he said.

"Hey, now don't get ideas," I said. "I'm not that kind of a girl. Anyway, you can probably sleep on the sofa in the living room after Dad's gone."

Frank headed for the garage, and I went inside and upstairs to get some blankets. When I walked into my bedroom, Dagmar sat straight up and asked. "What in the world has been going on around this place tonight? I've been trying to study, and I keep hearing all this screaming and fighting. You and Mom get into it again?"

Without answering I pulled a blanket out of the closet.

"What are you doing with that?" Dagmar demanded.

"Oh, I can't sleep, so I thought I'd watch the late show. It's a little chilly down there. Maybe I'll even sleep down there tonight."

I hurried out so she wouldn't give me the third degree. In a hall closet I found another blanket and headed for the garage.

Frank already had found the sleeping bag and had it laid out on the floor. I threw the two blankets down on it, but before I could spread them out, Frank grabbed me and kissed me. I just melted in his arms.

"Why don't you stay out here to keep me company?" he asked. "I'm afraid of the dark."

I gently pushed him away, saying, "Frank, please don't ask me that again. I'm just not into that kind of thing. Okay?"

"Come on, Denise; I won't touch you."

He started pulling me toward the sleeping bag. I knew I would be no match for his strength, so I pleaded, "Please, Frank, I'm not that kind of girl!"

"Denise, you're not such an angel," he countered. "You smoke pot. Come on. Why don't you spend the night? You might just really enjoy it!"

I wasn't so gentle as I pulled away now. No way was I going to get into that kind of trouble! Being pregnant and unmarried would be horrible! I couldn't face that!

"Frank, you listen to what I say," I ordered. "You'll stay here in the garage until I come out to get you in the

morning. I won't come out until I know the way is clear.
And if Dad leaves late, I'll bring some breakfast out to
you. But if my old man finds out you're here, he'll call
the cops again. And if I'm not in the house, he'll come
out here looking for me. Then we'll both be in deep
trouble."

"I guess you're right," Frank agreed reluctantly. "I'd
better stay cool."

At that moment I really wanted to kiss Frank good
night. But I was afraid of what it might lead to. There
was too much at stake tonight!

When I got back in the house, I walked upstairs and
started getting ready for bed. Dagmar was still awake
and wanted to know, "What's the matter? Wasn't the
movie any good?"

"No, it was too scary."

That seemed to satisfy her, and she turned over. By
her rhythmic breathing I could tell she was asleep.

I crawled into bed and lay there staring at the ceiling,
trying to sort out all the things that had happened tonight. Had I found my true love? Would Mom let Frank
stay with us? And what would that lead to if we were together all the time?

I turned and tossed and tossed and turned, trying to
make some sense out of it all. Was pot really the answer
to the problems and frustrations of life? I had to admit it
did make me feel good.

When I finally awoke, it was light outside. Dagmar
was gone. So was Philip. I looked at the clock. No wonder they were gone. It was about time for classes to start.
I'd be late again.

Nobody was around downstairs. I wondered if Dad
had left yet, or if it was safe for me to bring Frank in.

I headed back to my parents' bedroom and knocked. I
heard Mom grunt, so I asked, "Is Dad here?"

"No, he left about three this morning."

Good! Now I could bring Frank in.

He was still sound asleep, so I kissed his cheek, shook him gently, and called, "Wake up, Prince Charming. It's safe for you to come in now."

He sat up, stretched, and hugged me gently. Hand in hand we walked into the kitchen, and I fixed him some breakfast. I felt so housewifely, taking care of him. Maybe it wouldn't be too bad spending the rest of my life with Frank. If I could just reform him so he wouldn't get in trouble with the law. . . . That probably happened because of the way his parents treated him anyway.

I think Mom must have suspected what was going on, for soon she was down in the kitchen too. I don't ever remember her getting up before ten-thirty before. When she saw Frank, she grinned and asked, "Are you ready to make me happy again?"

Frank smiled back, but he said, "Sorry, Mrs. Brady; I don't have any pot. I guess I'm going to have to do something to get us some, hey?"

"Why don't you just go out and buy some?" I asked. "Then the three of us can smoke pot together."

Frank shrugged. "I don't have any money."

I suspected where he was getting his money, but the way I was falling for this guy, I wanted to know for sure. So I said, "How does one get money to buy pot?"

Frank laughed. "No problem. You get a job, and you work hard. With the money you earn, you buy pot."

"What kind of a job do you have, Frank?"

"Oh, I got laid off of the job I had after school," he said lamely. "But while I was still at home, I used to have a really good job, and I was able to put a lot of money in the bank."

"How much money, Frank?"

He pushed back from the table and studied me. "What are you driving at, Denise?"

"Oh, I thought I'd buy some pot myself," I said. "But I'm broke. I was wondering how I might get some money."

I still hadn't gotten a straight answer from Frank. Where did he get his money? Last night he said that weirdo he had been living with gave him money.

Mom moved over behind Frank's chair and patted his shoulder. "I believe you, Frank," she said. "You've been telling us the truth all along, haven't you?"

"Of course, Mrs. Brady. You can always trust what I tell you."

I knew differently, but I wasn't going to say so at this moment.

"I've got ten dollars," Mom offered. "Can that get us some?"

"Sure. I can buy ten joints for that!"

Mom headed back up to her bedroom for the money. While she was gone, I whispered, "Frank, I'm sorry I questioned you so much, but I do hope you're not making a habit out of breaking into houses and stealing to support your pot habit. You're not doing that, are you?"

"Denise, you're really stupid. You think I have a rich uncle or something? You know my folks are on welfare."

"That's not what I mean, Frank. I want to know straight out. Do you break into houses and steal to get money to buy pot?"

"Just as I said, you are stupid."

"Frank, quit calling me stupid. I told you that really aggravates me. And please answer my question. Do you break in houses and steal?"

Frank laughed. "Of course I do. I told you that in the pizza place last night. A person's got to do something to get the money to buy pot."

"What about that caper last night?" I pressed.

"Hey, wait a minute. I didn't pull off that one last night. I was with you. Remember?"

"Then who did it?"

"Listen, Denise, you've been living in a closed-up cage all your life, haven't you? There's all kinds of kids in this town who are on drugs. Some are smoking pot. Some are popping pills. I know some who are drilling themselves with heroin. Others are into the most expensive habit—snorting cocaine. I mean, it's everywhere. And all these kids need money for their drugs."

It was everywhere? Even I had smoked pot now. So had my mother. What were we getting into?

I'd better stop right now, while I still could. Or was it already too late? Was I going to end up a junkie?

5

When Mom returned waving the ten-dollar bill, she hit me with, "Denise, why haven't you left for school? You can't afford to miss again. Now you just run along. You hear me?"

I knew what she was getting at. She wanted to be alone with Frank. How disgusting! Frank wouldn't try anything with her, would he? Somehow I knew I couldn't be sure.

"I think I'll just stay home today," I responded. "I really don't feel too good, and—"

"Oh, no you don't!" she exploded. "You're not about to pull that one on me again. You get out of this house now before I call your principal and tell him you're cutting classes again!"

"I'll tell you what; let me walk you to school," Frank offered, trying to ease the situation.

"No, Frank, that won't be necessary," Mom announced. She came over and patted me, then said sarcastically, "She's a big girl now and can cross the street all by herself!"

Mother's tactics were so obviously transparent that it almost made me vomit. My dad was just barely out of the house, and already she was trying to make it with a teenager!

"No, I want to make sure she gets there all right," Frank told Mother. "Then I'll be right back."

"Frank, don't go!" Mother implored.

He snatched the ten dollars from her hand, winked at her, and said, "I'll walk her to school and then go meet my connection. It's not far from school where I get my pot."

"Oh, good!" Mom exclaimed. "Hurry right back!"

In disgust I grabbed my schoolbooks and headed out the front door. I couldn't stand the idea of the two of them at home smoking pot and doing who knows what else while I suffered through a boring day of classes.

"Hey, slow down, will you?" Frank called from behind me. "You're not that anxious to get there, are you?"

"Frank, you make me puke!" I said. "This whole thing's disgusting."

"Hey, baby, don't act that way. I haven't done anything wrong."

"Yeah, but I know what you've got in mind," I replied, not even turning to face him. "I listened to what you two were talking about. Now that you two have got it on, you can just jolly well forget about me."

How did I ever get myself into such a mess? Maybe Dad was right in not wanting Frank at our house. Maybe I should have gone with Dad to Wichita. Or maybe I just ought to run away. Nothing I touched seemed to work out right.

Frank finally caught up with me and grabbed my

arm. A little out of breath, he panted, "Hey, stop here just one minute, will you?"

I jerked away and snorted, "Get your slimy hands off me!"

Frank pulled his hand back and said gently, "I know you're upset. I can understand that. Your old lady is making an obvious play for me. But let me tell you something. I hate her just as much as you hate her!"

I stopped and looked into his eyes. "Really?" I asked.

"Listen, Denise, old men and old ladies are all alike. They have us as babies. When we get older, they can't handle us, and they really want us out of their hair. But they're really the babies! I've never yet met an old man or old lady who could handle kids. But I've met a lot of kids who knew how to handle their parents—me included. You are really stupid, Denise. All I was doing was setting your mom up."

"What do you mean?"

"Well, I got a place to stay, right?"

"Yeah."

"And I got ten bucks for ten sticks of pot." He waved the bill around. "I had to set her up to get that."

So Frank was leading her on so she would buy the pot!

"Another thing," Frank went on, "is that I'm going to teach you a lesson, a big lesson."

I was listening, but I wasn't quite sure about trusting any lesson I learned from Frank.

"Have your folks got any valuables?" he asked.

I laughed at the ridiculousness of his question. "You call me stupid?" I asked. "You were there. Couldn't you tell my folks are among the poorest of the poor?"

"Hey, let me tell you a few things about poor," Frank replied. "Some of these people, supposedly poor, have got money. I've been in their houses and found expensive jewelry."

"Jewelry? The only thing we've got is an old necklace my mom wears when she wants to dress up. But it's not worth anything at all."

"Is it gold?"

"I guess so. It looked like gold. But I know it's not worth anything."

"How can you be sure?"

"Listen, Dad bought that for her years ago—before I was born. They never had any money, even in those days. I bet he paid next to nothing for it."

"What he paid for it really doesn't make any difference now," Frank told me. "Don't you know the price of gold has gone through the roof? Those cheap gold things people bought years ago are worth a fortune today. I'll bet I could get at least fifty bucks for that old necklace."

"Frank, you've got to be off your rocker!"

"I'd sure like to take a look at it. Where does she keep it?"

"Frank, you're not going to rob my house, are you?"

"Denise, will you wise up? You don't live in a house; you live in a dump. Your old man and old lady have been mean to you. Your old lady beats you up. If I took that necklace, I'd be doing you a favor because I'd share the money with you too."

"Frank, you could get in trouble with the cops!" I warned. "You know what happened last night."

Frank laughed at the idea. "Let me tell you something else, Denise. The best place to rob is your own home."

"But, Frank, if I took that, Mom would come right to me as soon as she realized it was missing."

"Sure. And all you have to say is that you don't know anything about it."

"Frank, you don't know my mom. She never believes a word of anything I tell her. Even if you stole it, she'd blame me."

"That's what I'm trying to get at," Frank said. "Even

if she's convinced you stole the necklace, what is she going to do about it? She won't go to the cops and squeal on you. Get wise. Parents never call the cops on their own kids. It's too embarrassing for them."

Frank made it sound so convincing. I knew Mom wouldn't call the cops on Dagmar or Philip. But I think she might delight in calling them on me!

"Even if she says she's going to call the cops," Frank went on, "all you have to do is say, 'Go ahead, Mom. And as soon as they come, I'm going to have them bust you for smoking pot.' You've got something on her; use it. That'll scare her out of any notion of turning you in."

Frank laughed at his own cleverness, and I laughed too. I really did have power over Mother now. I could blackmail her if she got out of line!

"I'll tell you what, Frank," I said, latching onto his idea. "Why don't we plant some pot in the house? Then if she calls the cops, we can let them know she keeps pot in the house. They'll get a search warrant, find the pot, and then bust her. That'll keep her out of my hair for a long time. Isn't that a great idea?"

Frank playfully punched my arm as he said, "Great idea! I think we ought to form a partnership. Between the two of us, they'd never catch up with us. But let's get the necklace before we start wasting any pot. Okay?"

"I still think that necklace is worthless, Frank."

"You let me take care of that part," he said.

I glanced at my watch and Frank asked, "Are you really going to school?"

"I guess I have to."

"Come on, Denise, you're too smart for that. You don't have to go to school. What can they do about it if you don't go? Kick you out? Anyway, school is for dummies."

"What do you mean by that?"

"Listen, all I go to school for is to keep my cover,"

Frank said. "I can make contacts and get a little money at school. And when I get money, I can get pot. What else is there to life?"

Frank's analysis of life sounded too flip, but I really had nothing to disprove his statement. Maybe the only worthwhile thing was pot. I sure was looking forward to having it again.

"What else have you got valuable in your house?" Frank asked.

"Nothing that I know of."

"Got any sterling silver?" Frank pressed. "Or maybe some antiques—even up in the attic?"

"Frank, I guess I haven't made it clear to you. We're poor. My old man's been off work more than he's been on; now he's off in Wichita. We hardly have enough money for food. How could we afford sterling silver? There isn't anything I know of but that necklace."

"Well, that will do for starters. But keep your eyes open. If your old lady leaves her purse around, check it out. Maybe there'll be some money in it.

"Come on with me, and we'll have fun," Frank coaxed. "Let's forget school."

It didn't take much urging for me to turn away from school. Besides, I really wanted to be with Frank. And if I were with him, he wouldn't be alone with my mother!

"Are you going to get some pot now?" I asked.

"Why not?"

"Where do you get it?"

"Not too far from here. You know Visi's Junkyard?"

"I know where it is," I replied, "but I've never been there. I've heard my dad say he was going there to get parts."

"Well, old man Visi's got all kinds of junk," Frank told me. "Nobody would ever suspect him of being a pusher. Besides, he's smart. He hides pot in old wrecked cars. If he hears about a bust, he just sets those cars afire, and all the evidence is destroyed. Pretty smart, hey?"

When we walked into the office, Frank asked the young guy behind the desk, "Where's old man Visi?"

Without even looking up, the guy answered, "Out back."

"Out back" was a pretty general term. We spent a few minutes searching among the wrecks until we finally spotted an older man bent over a fender and peering under the hood of a wreck. Frank went up and swatted him on the seat of the pants.

The old guy jumped, then smiled when he saw Frank.

"Hey, Mr. Visi, I want you to meet a friend of mine," Frank said.

The old man rubbed his grimy hands on a grimier cloth, looked me up and down, and asked, "You sure this is a real friend of yours?"

"Yeah, man, she's cool. You can trust her."

"What's her name?"

"Denise Brady."

"Denise Brady? Is she Cecil's girl?"

Frank nodded.

Old man Visi stuck out his grimy hand and said, "Pleased to meet you, Denise. Oh, my! I never would have believed it!" He looked me over carefully again. "So you're Denise Brady."

I had no intention of shaking his filthy hand, but he grabbed mine and started pumping. "For years I've wanted to meet you," he said. "You really are a beautiful young lady."

Why would he want to meet me? And who had told him about me? Frank hadn't come here last night, had he?

"How do you know about me, Mr. Visi?" I asked.

He took the dirty rag and started wiping his hands again. But he didn't answer.

Then he began to laugh. Finally he said, "Ever hear of Salvatore Visi?"

Salvatore Visi? I didn't know anybody named Visi.

"No sir," I replied.

Mr. Visi laughed again. "Oh, I think you do. At least you must have heard about him."

"Well, I don't remember it. Is he a relative of yours?"

"My brother. He got killed in a motorcycle accident a few years back. He was always a daredevil."

"I'm sorry to hear he died," I said.

"Thank you, miss. Your mother's name is Harriet, isn't it?"

I nodded.

"Hasn't your mother ever told you about my brother?"

I shook my head, suddenly becoming terribly curious.

"Oh, sixteen, maybe seventeen years ago," Mr. Visi said, "Harriet left your old man and lived with my brother for a while."

Sixteen or seventeen years ago? That was about the time I was born! I stood there almost in shock. Was Mr. Visi trying to tell me that my real father was his brother Salvatore?

Frank must have caught my bewildered, frightened expression and said, "Mr. Visi, I came for ten sticks of pot. Here's ten bucks."

Mr. Visi pulled out a big wad of pot, counted off ten sticks, and exchanged them for the money. Then Frank grabbed my arm and said, "Let's get out of here."

I was still staring at Mr. Visi. Almost incoherently I asked, "What are you trying to tell me, Mr. Visi?"

He laughed as he said, "I'm not trying to tell you anything, kid. But you're sure a cute little thing."

Frank kept tugging at my arm. I tried to say something, but Frank jerked me away and soon ushered me out of the junkyard and onto the sidewalk outside.

"Was I hearing him right, Frank?" I asked. "Was he trying to tell me that his brother is my real father?"

"Denise, don't pay any attention to that old man. I mean, he's crazier than a cracker."

"I know you're trying to protect me, Frank. But for some time now I've been aware of some strange things going on in my family. My mother loves Philip, and she loves Dagmar, but she hates me! I've wondered if I were adopted. But what old man Visi said makes sense. The reason Mom hates me is that I'm illegitimate. Whenever she sees me, it reminds her of her affair."

"Come off it, Denise. Lots of kids think their parents aren't their real parents. But it's not true."

"Listen, Frank, there are also a lot of women who have shacked up with guys and gotten pregnant. That happens every day."

"Sure it happens. But that doesn't mean it happened to your mom. Don't listen to old man Visi. He's a crackpot. Next time we go back, he'll insist he was the one who had an affair with your mother and that you're his daughter. I mean, the old man's crazier than a loon."

I wasn't about to accept Frank's easy explanation. I had to know for sure. But I couldn't see any point in talking to him about it.

"Why don't you go on home, Frank," I suggested. "I think I need to walk around and think about all this."

"Listen, Denise, this whole thing is ridiculous. You're no more illegitimate than I am."

I wasn't sure I liked his metaphor, but all I said was, "Frank, I need some breathing room. You go on. Besides, Mom will be waiting for her pot."

"Okay, have it your way," he replied.

"Can I trust you with my mother, Frank?"

"For crying out loud, you can trust me. I'm not going to try anything with her. She's probably full of disease anyhow. What I want most is to get my hands on that necklace."

Frank took off for our house, and I wandered around here and there for the rest of the day, troubled over whether or not Mr. Visi was telling me the truth. If there were only some way I could find out. . . .

About the time school let out I headed home. But neither Mother nor Frank were around anywhere. When Dagmar came home and walked up to our bedroom, I followed her. She shut the door behind us and said mysteriously, "Denise, there's something I want to talk to you about."

One look at her face told me this was going to be serious.

"Denise, I was checking into this Frank at school today. The readings I get are that he is no good. And with Dad gone and Frank living here, I get the feeling something terribly wrong is going on."

"Hey, Dagmar, don't sweat it. Frank's a nice boy. He had no place to go, so I talked to Dad about this before he left. He said Frank could stay here. Mom likes him too."

"Did you know he's been kicked out of school five times?" Dagmar asked. "Right now he's on indefinite suspension."

"Come on, Dagmar, show a little compassion. He's got nowhere to go!"

"Denise, we need to talk about sense, not compassion," she countered. "The boy's no good. I understand he smokes pot. Some kids think he's pushing pot. If he stays here, he may try to get you on that terrible stuff. I understand from some of the kids that sometimes when someone starts pot, they just can't put it down. From there they go on to hard drugs. You don't want to take that kind of chance, do you? We've got to get rid of that turkey. I'm worried."

"You get rid of him, you get rid of me!" I shouted, stomping my foot. "If Frank goes, I go."

"Okay, okay," she replied, backing off. "But I don't like it one little bit."

"Look, Dagmar," I said, "I appreciate your concern for me. But there's something else I really need to talk to you about."

"Did that dirty Frank get you pregnant?"

"For crying out loud, Dagmar, you know I'm not that kind of a girl. I ought to slap you for thinking such things about me."

"Well, the way you've been acting the last day or two, I'd believe almost anything," she replied.

"Well, I'm not pregnant."

"Okay, then what's the problem?"

"It's about me. This afternoon I happened to run into old man Visi—from Visi's Junkyard, you know? Well, he acted as though he had been waiting to see me for years. He claims that his brother Salvatore, who is dead, is my real father."

As I was talking, I kept looking at Dagmar's eyes for signs that she might know what I was talking about. When I mentioned Salvatore Visi, she looked away from me.

I grabbed her and said, "Dagmar, you've got to tell me the truth. Is Dad really my dad?"

She tried to back away, but I shook her. "Tell me the truth, Dagmar! Tell me the truth!"

"I have no idea what you're talking about," she replied. "I've never heard of any of these people."

"You're lying, Dagmar. I can tell it. Look me in the eye and say you don't know!"

She pulled away and started to walk out the door. But I grabbed her shoulder and spun her around. "I'm not through yet, Dagmar," I shouted. "You know something that I need to know. Don't hold it back from me. Please! Please!"

She looked at me momentarily, then her eyes shifted again. I shook her once more and pleaded, "Please, Dagmar. I've got to know. Is Dad really my dad? Or is it that Salvatore? I sense what's going on in this house. You're loved; Philip is loved; but Mom hates me. Why? Why? Is it because I remind her of something she'd rather forget?"

Just then our bedroom door flew open, and there stood Mother demanding, "What's all the shouting about in here?"

I let go of Dagmar and looked into Mom's eyes. She was high.

"Denise and I were just having a little chat," Dagmar told her.

Mom wagged her finger in my face and said, "Young lady, you get downstars right away and clean up that kitchen. You do all those dishes. You left them again this morning. You're supposed to do those before you go to school."

I wanted to scream at her, "Is Dad my real dad? Am I being mistreated because I am illegitimate?" But I knew I'd never get the truth out of her. She might say I was illegitimate just to hurt me—even if it wasn't true.

"Mom, I'll go down there in just a minute. But I've got to talk to Dagmar a minute. Okay?"

I held my breath. Would she leave us alone?

Dagmar had been studying Mom's appearance and chose this moment to ask, "Is something the matter with you, Mom? Something about you looks strange. It looks as though it's your eyes."

Should I blurt out that she was high? Maybe I should save that revelation for when I could get more mileage out of it. So I added, "Mom, you really don't look well.

Why don't you go lie down until suppertime?"

I gently pushed her toward the door, and she stumbled out, mumbling something as she went.

"Okay, Dagmar, this is it!" I said when Mom was in her own room. "Either you tell me what you know about me, or I'm running away from home. I've got to know the truth!"

She stood there open-mouthed at my threat. So I said, "Tell me what you know, or tell me good-bye. This will be the last time you see me like this. I'm going to run away, and then I'm going to kill myself. I've got to know the truth!"

She still stood there staring at me, her mouth open. Did Dagmar know something about my beginnings? And if she did, would she ever tell me?

6

Dagmar swallowed hard. Avoiding my gaze, she looked first at the floor, then at the ceiling, then back to the floor.

I grabbed her and demanded, "Dagmar, tell me!"

She slowly pushed my hands off her shoulders, paced back and forth a few times, and then said thoughtfully, "Okay. Sit down. Maybe it's time for you to know."

In dread of what this terrible revelation held for me, I sat on the edge of my bed, wringing my hands. Dagmar sat opposite me on her bed, struggling to find the right words, the right way to tell me what she had to say.

"Denise," she started in, "if I tell you this, you've got to promise that you'll never tell Mom or Dad that I told you. Okay?"

"Okay! Okay!" I answered nervously. "Anything. Just tell me!"

"Well, I hope you're mature enough to take this. It's

hard enough for me to tell it; I know it'll be rough on you to hear it."

I wanted to reach over and strangle the truth out of her. Why was she beating around the bush like this? Why didn't she just tell me? But I knew I'd better restrain my emotions or she would change her mind and not tell me anything at all!

"A little while before you were born, Mom and Dad had some problems," she said. "Mom accused Dad of a bunch of things—of drinking, of being unfaithful."

"How do you know all that? You couldn't have been more than two years old!"

"I didn't know it, then, but there was a lot of talk about things later when I did understand."

"So what happened? Mom is always accusing Dad of something."

"Well, this time she took off and moved in with a guy."

"A guy?" I questioned. "Do you know who it was?"

"Salvatore Visi."

"Salvatore Visi?" I exploded. "That's the name that junk dealer told me today. Are you sure?"

"Yes, I'm sure," Dagmar answered. "And while Mom was living with him, she got pregnant. So what you suspected is true. Dad is not your real dad. Salvatore Visi is your father."

I sat there for a moment reeling under the revelation. Could this possibly be true?

"Dagmar, are you telling me the truth?" I demanded. "Or are you just doing this as some sort of a weird joke? Because if you are, I don't think it's at all funny."

"This is no joke, Denise," she said as kindly as she could. "I kept hearing rumors about this while I was growing up. And Leona, our older cousin, dropped a hint about it to me when I was about twelve. I went over to see Salvatore Visi after that, and he just laughed and laughed when I asked him about it. He thought it was all a big joke. I was planning to go see him again sometime, but shortly after that he was killed in a motorcycle accident."

"Why didn't you tell me this before?" I demanded.

"You weren't ready for it. Besides, I didn't think it would do any good. After all, what's done is done. You are here, and Dad treats you just as though you were his own. Fatherhood is more than biological, you know."

I sat there trying to absorb the implications of what Dagmar had been telling me. Now I knew why my mother hated me—because I had been born as a result of a filthy relationship she had had with a junk dealer! Oh, how I wanted to scratch her eyes out for what she had done!

"So help me, Dagmar, I'm going to get her for this, if it's the last thing I do!" I spluttered.

"Take it easy, Denise. There is nothing you can do about it. You can't change the facts. You might as well just try to make the best of it."

"That's what you think!" I shouted. "I'm going to pay her back for what she did to me! She is going to be sorry!"

"What do you have in mind?"

"I don't know yet. I might even kill her!"

"Come on, Denise, what good would that do? If you kill your mother, you'll go to the slammer for murder—maybe even be electrocuted. Cold-blooded murder isn't going to change the fact that Salvatore Visi was your father."

I stared straight at her and said, "You go ahead and be so self-righteous. You've got a mother and a father. My father is dead! How do you think I feel about all this?"

"I'll bet you feel horrible, just horrible," she replied sympathetically. "I can understand that. I know how I would feel if I were in your place."

Maybe Dagmar did understand. But I was still mad—mad at my old lady, mad at Salvatore Visi, mad at the world.

Waving my arms wildly, I jumped up and headed for the bedroom door. Dagmar jumped up and started after me, yelling, "Where are you going?"

"Where do you think I'm doing? I'm going to find my old lady and punch her right in her big mouth! That's what I'm going to do!"

Before I got to the door, Dagmar had grabbed me and pulled me back. "Denise, you start slapping Mom around," she warned, "and she'll take into you. You know you're no match for her strength. You saw that yesterday!"

Something was churning inside me—hate, loathing, anger—and I looked straight at Dagmar and spit out the words: "Don't you be so self-righteous. Knowing Mother's morals, you're probably illegitimate too! There's no telling who your old man is!"

"When I found out about you, that thought occurred to me too," she answered calmly. "So I went down to the city hall to check the birth records."

"And?"

"I'm Daddy's girl."

"What about me. Did you check my record?"

"Yes, I did."

"Well, what did you find out?" I asked, almost dreading to hear what I knew she was going to tell me.

"Salvatore Visi is listed as your father."

"What?" I yelled. "How could she do that to me? Why couldn't she have had the decency at least to list Dad as my father?"

Dagmar shrugged. "You know Mom. She probably saw it as a way of getting even with Dad."

That was it! I pulled away from Dagmar's loose grip and bolted out the door. My old lady was going to get it now!

She was down in the living room watching TV. "Mom!" I screamed.

She didn't look around or answer me—just stared straight ahead blankly at the TV.

I'd show her! I ran into the kitchen, grabbed the biggest butcher knife I could find, ran back into the living room, and screamed, "Mom, look here!"

Still no response. How could she ignore me like this?

The hatred and anger I felt broke something inside of me, and I leaped toward her, grabbed her hair, and jerked it backwards. Holding the point of the knife just inches from her throat I announced, "I'm going to kill you, you filthy woman!"

Her mouth flew open, and her eyes bugged out in fright. I'd never seen that look on her face before. She was scared to death!

"Tell me the truth!" I demanded. "Who is my father?"

"What in the world's gotten into you?" she stuttered. "You're off your rocker. Now put down that butcher knife this instant or you're going to be sorry!"

"You're the one who's going to be sorry!" I returned, touching the point of the knife to her throat.

"Denise Brady, put down that knife!" she ordered. "You're hurting me!"

"Not nearly as much as you're hurting me!" I retorted. "Now tell me, Mrs. Brady, who is my real father?"

"Why, Cecil is. He's your father. What's the big deal?"

"Then who is Salvatore Visi?" I demanded.

I was right up to her face, and when I mentioned that

name, she tried to avoid my gaze. But there was no way
she could do that since I had the knife at her throat. She
didn't have to tell me anything. That look told me all I
needed to know. I was illegitimate!

I jerked on her hair again, yelling, "Answer me!"

"Denise, I'll answer you," she said. "But first put
down that knife. I can't talk with that thing up against
my throat."

At the moment I felt like slashing her throat and getting this whole mess over with. But I guess I at least
owed her the chance to explain.

"Please put down the knife, Denise."

I guess that was the only time she had ever said
"please" to me, and I softened just a little. Somehow this
woman didn't seem like any kind of a mother to me. All
the years she had mistreated me. Now I knew why. She
was ashamed of me! Every time she saw me, it brought
back a sordid chapter in her life, a chapter she would
just as soon forget.

I pulled the knife away from her throat but still kept it
poised as I said, "Okay, talk. But you try anything foolish, and this knife goes right through your heart!"

Releasing my grip on her hair, I took a step backward
and demanded, "The truth, Mother! Who is my father?"

She moved her shoulders back and forth to try to re-
gain her composure and without looking directly at me
said, "Okay, Denise, I don't know where you got your
information, but you really are Salvatore Visi's girl."

"Why didn't you tell me before?" I demanded. "Why
didn't you tell me I was illegitimate?"

"Come on, Denise, quit trying to make a federal case
out of it. This happens in the best of families. Don't take
it so hard." Then she started to laugh.

I raised the knife again and shouted, "This is no
laughing matter, Mrs. Brady! This affects my whole
life!"

"Aw, grow up," she said disgustedly. "Cecil and I weren't getting along, and I met Salvatore in a bar. I went to his apartment that night and just decided to move in with him. I wanted and needed understanding right then, and he gave it to me. Well, nine months after I moved in with Salvatore, you were born. No problem."

"What do you mean, no problem?" I screamed. "Maybe that's no problem for you with all your sleeping around town, but what do you think it's doing to me to find out I'm illegitimate? And why couldn't you at least have listed Dad as my father on my birth certificate?"

"Oh, you saw that, eh?" she said. "Well, your dad and I still weren't back together when you were born. So why not tell the truth on the records?"

Then she started to laugh again. When I glared, she said, "Hey, I think the whole thing's kind of funny. Salvatore was a nice enough guy. Too bad you never got to meet him. He was killed in a motorcycle accident a few years back."

"So I found out today."

"Denise, don't take this so hard. It's not really all that bad."

I gritted my teeth and raised the knife higher. Maybe if I just slashed her face, then she'd carry a scar for the rest of her life as a reminder of the terrible thing she did to me. But somehow, I just didn't have the nerve.

As we stood there in that face-off, I heard someone coming up the front steps. Quickly I lowered the knife and put it behind my back. When that person knocked on the door, Mom and I looked at each other questioningly. I motioned for her to get up and answer it.

When she opened the door, there stood Frank. "Is Denise here?" he asked. Then glancing in, he saw me.

With the knife still in my hand, I backed toward the TV and let the knife drop behind it. I don't think he saw it.

"Young man, you are no longer welcome in this house!" Mom yelled, swearing at him. "I know all about you. Now you get out of here and don't ever come back again!"

Her change of attitude toward Frank really puzzled me. This morning she could hardly wait to be alone with him and get high. What could possibly have changed her attitude so quickly?

"Hey, why all the flak?" Frank asked.

"I said get out of here right now!" she ordered.

When Mom started pushing him back outside, I ran over, grabbed his arm, and tried to pull him back in.

"Denise, I don't want you to have anything more to do with this loudmouth!" Mom exploded. "I know he's the one who told you about Salvatore Visi!"

"No, Mom, he wasn't," I protested. "It wasn't Frank!"

"Look, I know better. I know he gets his pot from Salvatore's older brother. That had to be where this came out."

I started to blurt out that it was her precious Dagmar who told me, but I remembered I had promised Dagmar that I'd never let Mom know she had told me. There was no sense in getting her involved in this mess.

Mom was still pushing Frank. He had grabbed the doorposts, and she wasn't having much luck getting him out. But she was screaming and cursing and threatening, "Get out now, or I'll call the cops. If they come now and bust you, they'll probably find pot on you. And I'll tell them you've been selling it to me. There's a lot stiffer penalty for pushing than there is for possession!"

One glance at Frank's face told me he did have pot on him. He let go of the doorposts immediately and started backing away, saying, "Okay, have it your way, Mrs. Brady; I'm leaving now. But you're all wrong!"

"Frank! Wait for me!" I yelled.

But before I could get out the door, Mom grabbed

me, shouting, "You're not going with any filthy swine like—"

Jerking away I yelled, "Get your dirty hands off me. You've got no right to cast stones!"

I should have been ready, but it happened so quickly that it caught me by surprise. *Whap!* The back of her hand caught me right across the mouth. I reached up to rub it because of the pain, and when I pulled my hand back down, I saw the blood.

At that point I lost all sense of reason and lunged for her, yelling, "I'll kill you! So help me, I'll kill you!"

But as I lunged, I was tugged backward by someone jerking my hair. Why would Frank do that after the way she had treated him? Then I heard Dagmar's voice yelling, "Denise, that's enough! Get hold of yourself!"

It was a good thing Dagmar was there—and even better that I didn't still have that knife in my hand. If I had, it would have plunged through all that fat right into my mother's heart!

Jerking away from Dagmar, I ran out onto the porch, slammed the door viciously behind me, and threw myself into Frank's arms. He had been standing there observing the scene.

"What in the world is going on around here?" he asked in surprise. "I thought I was in your mom's good graces—and then this. What's happened?"

I pushed myself out of his embrace, grabbed his arm, and started pulling him down the steps. "Frank, you've got to get me away from here before I kill her!"

"Okay, so tell me what's the matter."

"I'm so angry, I don't know how to say it," I answered. "If I tell you, it'll make me angry all over again."

Frank laughed. "You're a real tiger, aren't you? I've never seen this side of you before. You sound as if somebody ripped off your pot."

"Frank, you know what old man Visi said this morning? Well, it's true. Salvatore Visi is my father. It's even on my birth certificate."

He laughed. "And that's what's got you all upset? Big deal!"

I doubled up my fist and let it go at his face. He saw it coming and ducked, grabbing my arm and twisting it as he did.

"Denise, for crying out loud, just stay calm, baby. Don't take your anger out on me. I had nothing to do with it."

"I warned you, Frank. Every time I think of it, it makes me furious. I want to fight. I want to kill. I want to destroy. I'm illegitimate. My old man was a junkyard bum!"

"Come on," he said, releasing his grip on my wrist and taking my arm gently. "I think you need something to solve your problems."

Frank pulled out a joint, lit it, and handed it to me. I inhaled, and then I felt it. Slowly the hatred within began to dissolve, and I began to feel peaceful. Maybe the whole thing wasn't such a big deal after all.

When we got through smoking the joint, I said, "Frank, I think I just did a terribly stupid thing. I've run away from home, and I have no place to go."

Frank threw his arms around me and said, "Baby, I know just the place where they'll take you in."

"Where?" I asked eagerly.

"Visi's Junkyard!" Then he cackled.

I pushed him away, shouting, "Frank, that's not funny! Don't you ever mention that name to me again! I couldn't help what my mother did, and you know it!"

"I guess that was kind of cruel," Frank admitted. "I won't bring it up anymore."

I looked into his eyes. They seemed to mirror kindness and understanding.

"Really, what am I going to do now?" I wailed.

"No problem."

"No problem? Here my world breaks apart, and everybody tells me it's no problem. Frank, be serious. It's a really big problem, and you know it! I can't go home. Just before you came, I threatened her with a butcher knife. If I go home, she'll call the cops on me. Maybe even have me admitted to a crazy house!"

"Wow, you do have a temper, don't you? It must be that Italian blood!"

"Frank, stop it!" I yelled. "You promised me you wouldn't bring that up again!"

"Sorry," he chuckled. "I guess I've got a weird sense of humor. Forgive me."

"Well, Frank, I do have a problem, whether you think so or not. I hate my mother, and she hates me. Now I realize why. I bet that every time she looks at me it reminds her of her past. And even my dad knows about it!"

"Why wouldn't he?" Frank said. "I had heard about it, and I didn't even know you."

"You mean the whole town knows about me?" I wailed.

"Denise, you know how people talk. But it doesn't mean anything. It's not your fault."

"Dad's always been so nice to me," I mused. "Maybe that's why. Maybe he was trying to make it up to me. He knew I would need extra love and security—especially with Mom treating me the way she did. Maybe that's why he showed extra attention to me."

"Could be."

"Frank, I wish he were here now instead of being off in Wichita. I really need to talk to him."

"Would I do as a substitute?" Frank asked. "I'm a good listener."

"Frank, I need more than a listener. I need a place to stay. Dad would help me with that."

"Denise, I've got a little surprise for you. I've been really busy today. After I left you, I went back to your house and smoked some pot with your mother. I could see she was getting amorous, so I made an excuse about taking care of some business and got out of there. I left her a few joints so she wouldn't be on my case.

"Then I was out wandering around, made some contacts, and was able to rent this apartment. When I came to your house just now, what I was really coming for was to see if you—"

"An apartment?" I interrupted. "Where did you get that kind of money?"

"Well, baby, don't tell anybody this, but I've been doing a little dealing on the side."

Oh, no! Dealing drugs. If Frank were to get busted for that, that would really be bad.

"Frank, aren't you worried about doing that?"

"What? Me worry?" he asked, making a ridiculous face. "It sure beats frying hamburgers at McDonald's!"

Frank gallantly took my arm and said, "Come with me to my little world. You don't have anywhere else to go now. Besides, I suspect you'd make a terrific little housewife!"

I went along because he was right—I had no place else to go. But what I was looking for was a place to stay—not a relationship. I didn't want to get into anything like that. I hardly knew Frank.

We walked down the block and Frank stopped by a car—a really sporty one—pulled out some keys, and unlocked the door.

I looked at him puzzled and asked, "Is this yours?"

"Sure is, baby; that's something else I did today. I bought this car. Isn't it a dandy?"

"Frank, it's fantastic!" I exclaimed, sliding inside.

"I got a great deal on it," Frank told me when he got behind the wheel.

Wow! Things were really looking up! I had Frank, his apartment, and his car!

We drove to a nearby community and a fairly new apartment complex. *How can Frank afford something like this?* I wondered.

After he parked the car, we went up to the second floor, and he ushered me into a small but beautiful apartment. I couldn't believe it. It was spic and span—totally unlike the dump I had lived in. And it had fantastic new contemporary furnishings. It looked like a page out of *Better Homes and Gardens!*

"Frank, where did you get the money for all this?" I asked suspiciously.

"Some guy got transferred," he told me. "He said he worked for IBM and that it was cheaper for him to sell his furniture than to move it all. He gave me a deal you wouldn't believe."

"Frank," I said, pressing him, "when you were at our house this morning, you didn't have a buck for a joint. How come—"

Instead of answering, he grabbed my hand and gave me a guided tour of the three-room apartment. Whoever had lived here before sure had good taste. Most of the furniture was almost new and had been taken care of. I didn't ever dream I'd get to live in a place like this!

But as I toured the apartment, I realized there was only one bedroom. That scared me.

"Where am I going to sleep?" I asked.

Frank pointed to the bedroom.

"Oh, no you don't!" I protested. "I told you I'm not that kind of a girl. That isn't why you brought me here, is it?"

"Well, you can't blame a guy for trying to make it with a beautiful brunette!" he exclaimed. "But you can sleep out here in the living room. The sofa pulls out into a bed."

Sighing deeply in relief, I said, "Thanks for being understanding, Frank." I didn't want to blow it. I really would like to live here. And I could do a lot of things to help out. But I wasn't interested in being any man's mistress.

"Can I be your cook and housekeeper?" I asked.

"Why not?" he answered. "If I'm going to provide this nice apartment for you to live in, you'll have to do something to pull your weight."

"No problem on that score," I said. "I used to be a chef at a famous French restaurant in New York City."

"*Oui!*" Frank exclaimed. "And I bet your ancestors were French, not Italian?"

"Frank, let's get something straight!" I exploded. "You promised to forget that subject. Let's just say I'm Irish. Okay?"

"Well, you've got the temper for that!" he replied. "But, Denise, you and I have to have an understanding. I've had a bad beginning like you've had a bad beginning. If I make a joke about something, it's not to put you down or hurt you. It's just my way of trying to be funny."

Maybe I was too sensitive. "Okay, Frank, I'll try to be understanding about it. It's a deal. You can even call me your little *mama mia*, if you want. Whatever you say like that, I'll take as a joke."

He threw his arms around me and kissed me. I could have stayed there forever, so secure in his arms. Yet down deep I knew this couldn't last. It didn't fit for a teenager to be penniless in the morning and to have a car, an expensive apartment and furniture by evening. We had to be heading for a day of reckoning, and I figured it wouldn't be long.

7

"Do you like the apartment?" Frank asked.

"Oh, yes! Yes!" I enthused. "It's what I've always dreamed of!"

"It's a lot nicer with you here," he told me, smoothing back my hair. "Ever since it started to work out today, I've been scheming about how I was going to get you over here with me. And that old slob of a mother of yours just pushed you right into my arms! What else could a man ask for?"

"Well, there are some things you'd better not ask for!" I announced, pushing away from him.

"Okay, I get that message loud and clear," he said. "So how about getting started on some of the things you will do—such as fixing my supper?"

"Coming right up, sir! How about frozen pizza? That's what I do best!"

We both laughed, and Frank said, "Well, we'd better

go shopping. That's one thing I didn't have a chance to get done today. Besides, I don't know anything about it. That's why I went to your house first, hoping—"

"Well, I don't know much about it either," I told him. "But we can learn together. I always just got what my mother sent me after. That always included some junk food for her, the old fat slob!"

We laughed together, and I thought, *This isn't going to be bad at all!* I didn't remember hearing much laughter around our house recently.

On the way to the supermarket, Frank pointed to a small store. "Look over there, Denise."

"I don't see anything unusual."

He pulled to the curb directly in front and pointed to the HELP WANTED sign.

"There's a job for you, baby," he said.

"Hey, Frank, I didn't say I wanted a job. I agreed to be a housewife. Surely you don't expect me to cook, clean the apartment, and work too! That's slavery!"

"Baby, this won't just be work. I went in there today to get a pack of cigarettes, and I came up with a great scheme."

"But I don't know the first thing about grocery stores," I protested.

"No problem. Baby, they told me they're looking for someone to work evenings—from six until ten. That means four hours a night, and only four days a week. Pretty simple, hey?"

"Come on, Frank. I can't tell when you're kidding and when you're serious. Do you really want me to work in there?"

"Well, they pay five dollars an hour. That's twenty dollars a night."

"That's not a lot of money for the way you're living."

"I know that. That's where my scheme comes in. I figured out how you can add another twenty dollars to that—maybe as much as fifty dollars. And it's a simple plan."

I figured what Frank was up to and said, "It would be dangerous to push pot in there—too many people coming and going. And somebody could be right here on the street like we are and watch what's going on inside."

"Hey, you think I'm stupid?" Frank asked. "No pushing in there. All you have to do is put your hand in the till."

"Put my hand in the till? What are you getting at?"

"I guess it's like robbery, only it's a lot safer because it's an inside job," he explained. "When no one is around, you just put your hand in the till—take some money out of the cash register—and slip it into your purse. Who's going to know you took the money? Even if they suspect it, how can they prove it? You just came up short at the end of the day—maybe gave somebody too much change. Baby, it's so simple that it can't lose!"

I looked inside. At that moment there was nobody in the store, and the clerk was just standing there. Frank was right. It wouldn't be too hard to slip out some money.

"Besides, whatever you get will be yours!" Frank offered magnanimously. Just think of all the nice clothes you can buy. We can go out to eat in expensive restaurants. We can have a big time—and it'll be so easy, baby."

With visions of new clothes floating through my brain, I said, "Wait here. I'll be right back!" and hurried off into the store. I walked up to the counter and watched as a customer checked out. The cash register was loaded with dough!

When that customer left, the man behind the counter said, "May I help you?"

"Yes, I saw your sign in the window. I've had a little experience working in a grocery store. You still need help?"

"Do I ever!" he responded. "I just can't seem to find anyone to work anymore. I don't know what's the matter, but there sure are a bunch of lazy bums running loose in this town."

"Well, I sure need work," I said. "I just got married, and I suppose you know how it is when you first start out. There's simply not enough money for all the things we need. So I asked my husband if it would be all right if I looked for a job."

"I know what you mean," the man said almost dreamily. "I remember when Emma and I first got married. Things were pretty rough. But we got along."

"How much does the job pay?" I asked.

"Well, five dollars an hour to start. But there's a little hitch."

"Oh?"

"The hours are from six to ten in the evenings, four nights a week. But it isn't hard work. You don't have to stock shelves or lift heavy boxes. But I do need someone here from six to ten Monday through Thursday."

"No problem," I told him. "In fact, those would be good hours for me. My husband works second shift anyway."

"Hey, this must be my lucky day!" The owner replied excitedly. "Would you be wanting to work for quite some time?"

I nodded, even though I had no idea of how long we would be around. All I was interested in was getting some money for some nice clothes.

"My name's Gene Shannon," the man said, extending his hand. "What's yours?"

"Denise Brady," I replied. Then I remembered I was

supposed to be married. "I mean Denise Burke," I corrected myself. "Oh, I'm so embarrassed. Brady was my maiden name."

He thought that was funny. Then he asked me when I could come to work.

"Oh, any time. How about tomorrow night?"

"Great! I need for you to fill out this application." He pulled one out from underneath the counter and handed it to me. "If you can fill it out now, it would be a little easier—"

"Maybe I'd better take it with me, if that's okay," I said. "I noticed it asks for things like my husband's Social Security number. I'm afraid I haven't memorized that yet. I have trouble remembering my name." Then I laughed.

"Sure, take it with you. No problem. And, Denise, I've got a feeling you're going to work out just fine!"

"Thanks, Mr. Shannon. See you tomorrow at six," I said and headed back to the car.

As we drove away, I told Frank I got the job. He laughed. "I'll bet you can talk your way into or out of anything," he said proudly. "Denise, you're quite a girl. When we get home tonight, I'll fill you in on some more details of my plan."

We bought a lot of groceries at the supermarket— certainly better than I had ever had before—including a big steak for our dinner. I was going to like living with Frank. And I liked the idea of having some money of my own too.

Frank set the table while I fixed the meal. And after we ate, he even offered to help me with the dishes. I couldn't get over how thoughtful and helpful he was. I was even entertaining the idea of our getting married and living happily ever after.

I snuggled up next to him on the sofa after dinner, and he said, "Denise, I need to tell you a little bit more about

that grocery-store deal. If anyone ever accuses you of
taking the money, deny it, and deny it vehemently. And
when you deny it, stare at the guy. Don't turn your eyes
to one side or the other. People who tell lies won't look
into other people's eyes. And don't just deny it. Tell
the guy you are going to sue him for falsely accusing
you. Sometimes these guys don't really know what's
going on, and they just sort of test you. But whatever
you do, don't play their game; make them play your
game."

The idea of ripping off a grocery store was beginning
to sink in, and my heart beat faster. Frank made it
sound so simple. Maybe it was going to be harder than I
expected.

Frank went back over the plan again, and then we sat
around watching TV. I got a little nervous when it was
time to go to bed and kept my eye on Frank when he
went into the bedroom. But he came back with some
sheets and blankets and said, "Here you go, baby; these
are for you."

I breathed a little easier. I couldn't even think of taking my clothes off in front of Frank.

I went into the bathroom, figuring I'd put on my pajamas in there. Then I remembered. I didn't have any
pajamas with me. I didn't even have a change of
clothing!

So I went back into the living room, shut off all the
lights, took off my jeans and blouse, and crawled into
bed. Tomorrow I would have to buy some clothes.
Maybe Frank would give me an advance until I got
some money from the cash register tomorrow. I noticed
he had quite a wad of money when he paid for the groceries. Where was it all coming from?

Then I decided it was silly to worry about it. He had
it, so why not live it up while we could? New clothes, a
nice apartment, a sporty car, good food—and Frank,

who, true to his word, stayed in his own bedroom with the door shut all night long.

Frank was gone for a little while the next day. I spent the time polishing all the furniture. I had a great meal fixed for Frank when he came home at four-thirty. He seemed so appreciative. Then after we washed the dishes, he drove me over to the grocery store where I was supposed to begin work.

Mr. Shannon immediately began explaining the job and showed me how the cash register worked. I listened carefully. I didn't want to blow this golden opportunity.

He spent the whole evening by my side, so there was no chance to rip off any money. I was nervous and made a few little mistakes, but he seemed quite patient with me. I guess he was glad for almost any help he could get.

The next evening Mr. Shannon told me he'd stay with me for an hour. "After that it won't be too busy," he said. "I think you can handle things fine. You seem to learn fast. And I'll be at home with my family, so you can reach me if you need me."

"Thanks, Mr. Shannon," I said. "I appreciate your confidence. I hope I'll do a good job and make a lot of money for you."

He laughed. "Well, there isn't a lot of money to be made in the grocery business," he said. "But I'm glad you're here so I can have a few hours off now and then."

He stayed until about eight. When he left, he took quite a bit of money out of the cash register, but he left some so I'd be able to make change.

I don't know what he was thinking about, saying that night wouldn't be very busy. There was hardly a minute when I wasn't ringing up a customer or checking on an item for somebody.

Finally at about 9:45 P.M. there wasn't a soul in the store but me. I punched the register and stood there looking at all that cash. Figuring it wouldn't be wise to take too much, I pulled out a twenty and stuffed it into my blouse.

When Frank picked me up, he asked how I was doing. When I told him I had taken only twenty dollars, he said, "That's smart, Denise. Start low and work up."

For the next three weeks I lifed a twenty every night I worked. Then I made it a twenty and a ten. Frank spent his time selling dope, and he often was out pushing while I was working in the store. I offered to quit the store and push dope too, but he thought it would be best for one of us to have a legitimate job. Besides, I was making pretty good money, and he was waiting until I was taking fifty dollars a night.

When I'd been working for about two months, I noticed Mr. Shannon didn't leave one night after I came in. I wondered about it but didn't ask—just kept busy waiting on customers.

When all the customers were gone and the store was empty, Mr. Shannon came over and said, "Denise, I seem to be missing some money. You know anything about it?"

"Missing some money?" I asked, faking shock. "There's been no robbery while I've been here!"

"I didn't say anything about a robbery. I just said I've been missing some money. Do you know anything about it?"

I remembered what Frank said, so I stomped my foot down hard and shouted, "Are you accusing me of taking your money?" I looked him straight in the eye, and he looked away. Maybe he was the one who was lying!

"Mr. Shannon, are you accusing me of stealing money from your store?" I demanded.

He grabbed my arm and pulled me along after him, saying, "Come here, you little twerp. I want to show you something."

I wanted to jerk away, and I probably could have. But I figured it would be better to hold steady. To run would be like an admission of guilt.

He marched me to the front door, pointed across the street, and said, "See that post office over there?"

"Of course I see it. It's been there a long time. What's that got to do with anything?"

"Young lady, my friend Jim Klosky is the postmaster over there. When I told him I thought I was being ripped off, he suggested I bring my camera with a telephoto lens on it over there at night. Denise, I've got pictures of you taking money out of the cash register."

He had me. But I remembered that Frank had warned me never to admit anything, so I said, "That's a likely story. Show me your pictures!"

"I can't. The police have them."

"You're lying, Mr. Shannon!" I shot back. "There are no pictures. No way can there be because I've never taken a dime from you!"

He yanked on my arm again, yelling, "I've got something else to show you, Denise."

This time I jerked away, shouting, "Don't you dare touch me! You are getting yourself into a peck of trouble. I'm going to have my husband's lawyer sue you for defaming my character!"

"Come with me!" he ordered.

I followed him back to the storeroom. He pointed up to the rafters and announced, "I laid up there and watched you steal money from my register too."

"You're lying!" I yelled. "I demand that right now you show me those alleged pictures. I demand you tell me exactly how much money I'm supposed to have taken. Maybe I gave the wrong change to customers, but I'm no common thief!"

"I can't be positive about how much you took," he

admitted. "There are frequently overages and shortages in this business. But I distinctly saw you take out a bill and stuff it into your blouse. I saw that, Denise!"

"Okay, Mr. Shannon, call the cops right now. Let's get this thing settled. No one is going to accuse me of stealing and get by with it!"

What would I do if he called my bluff and phoned the cops? My heart was beating like crazy. But somehow I figured he only had a suspicion—no proof.

"Go ahead. Call the cops! I'm waiting, Mr. Shannon."

He stared at me uneasily. "Denise, did you steal money from me?"

I stomped my foot again and shouted, "You dirty old man! I'll bet you're the one who's stealing. You don't want your wife to know it, do you? What's the matter? You keeping another woman somewhere? And now you want to lay the blame on me!"

I saw him grit his teeth as he snarled, "Why you filthy little crook! I know you're stealing from me!"

Next to me was an empty wooden box. I grabbed it and holding it over my head, shouted, "I ought to kill you for the way you're falsely accusing me."

"Put that down before I wrap it around your neck!" he threatened.

Figuring I was going too far, I slowly put down the box. But I figured I'd better find a way out while I still could.

Just then a customer walked in. I pointed at him and said, "You go wait on him, Mr. Shannon. I'm going to stay back here and watch to be sure you don't steal any money!"

"You're disgusting!" he hissed as he started up to the front.

As soon as he was busy with the customer, I slipped out the rear door, down the alley, and ran a few blocks until I came to a phone booth.

Frank answered, and I explained my predicament. "Where are you now?" he asked.

"Down about three blocks from the store on Maple— at a phone booth."

"Did you deny everything?" he asked.

"Yeah, I remembered everything you told me. He claims he has photographs taken from the post office across the street."

"Did you see the photos?"

"No, I demanded to see them, but he said the cops have them."

"Denise, you've got to get out of there right now!" Frank urged. "You're too close to the store. He's probably called the cops by now, and you'd be a sitting duck waiting in a phone booth that close to the store. Get out of there right now!"

I slammed down the receiver and took off. Dumb me! I should have at least told Frank where to look for me! But I didn't dare go back now.

I ran another direction for several blocks, then turned again, and spotted a gas station with a phone booth inside. I ran in and called Frank again.

"I'm at the Texaco station on Elm," I told him.

"I know right where that is. I'll be there in just a couple of minutes. But keep low."

I hung up and as casually as possible walked over to where a mechanic was changing the oil in a car. He looked up and asked, "Can I help you?"

"No thanks," I said. "My husband's coming after me here. I was walking home, and I think there was a guy following me. I kind of panicked."

He looked me up and down and said, "Well, you're a pretty good-looking kid. Can't say that I blame anybody for following you."

"Mister, you lay a hand on me, and I'll drop you with a wrench over the head!" I said with more bravado than I felt.

He laughed. "They can't send you to jail for looking," he said. "Besides, I like my women good looking and with a bit of spunk. You fit the bill, kid."

With that he leaned back over a fender and started tinkering with something in the car's engine. I breathed easier.

I paced back and forth nervously. And when I heard a siren, I almost jumped out of my skin!

The mechanic looked up and said, "Hey, what's the matter? The cops after you?"

"I don't know," I said. "Last week I got stopped for doing sixty in a twenty-five-mile zone. I always drive too fast, and that cop threatened to haul me in for reckless driving. I told him a big story to get out of it, but every time I hear the sirens now, I get nervous."

"Hey, that'll teach you, kid," he said, laughing. "My kid brother's like you—always speeding. One more ticket and they take away his driver's license."

I kept pacing, hoping that Frank would hurry up. When I saw a car approaching, I started outside to meet it. Too late I realized it was a cop car, pulling up into the station! And I had nowhere to hide!

A cop got out, came inside, nodded to me, and then said, "Hi, Hank. How are things going?"

"Just fine. Norman. What's up? Need some gas?"

"No, we just got a report about a robbery at a grocery store. You didn't see anybody run by here, did you?"

I kept staring out the window. Should I turn around and face the cop? Or should I just try to ignore what was going on? I didn't have to decide, when he called to me: "Young lady, did you see or hear anything this evening?"

"No, I sure didn't," I answered as coldly as I could.

He walked over and said, "What's your name?"

"Barbara Schwartz."

"Where do you live?"

"Hey, how come you're giving me the third degree?" I asked edgily. "I didn't rob any grocery store."

"Who said you did?" the officer asked.

"Look, I was just in here waiting for my husband," I explained. "I was walking home, and some guy started following me. I really got worried that he might try to rape me. So I came in here. Could you take me home?"

"You sure you're all right, ma'am?"

I realized then that I'd said a dumb thing. They could get me for making a false report. But I'd said it, and it was a little late to try to back out now. So I bent over and started to cry.

The officer touched my shoulder gently and said, "Hey, don't take it so hard. You're okay, aren't you?"

I tried heaving my shoulders, hoping the tears would come. Sure enough, they did. I didn't know I was such a good actress!

"Officer, I'm still scared to death," I said. "I called my husband to come and get me, but he's apparently been delayed somewhere. So can you take me home?"

"Sure," he replied kindly. "We're not working on that burglary case anyway—we just heard it on our radio. A couple of other officers are investigating that one. We'll be glad to take you home. You don't need to be afraid. We're here to protect you."

Just as we got outside and I started to get into the police car, Frank drove up. He stared open-mouthed. I knew what he was thinking—that the cops had busted me! If only there was some way I could let him know. But before I could say anything, he took off.

That didn't leave me much choice but to have the cops take me back to the apartment.

They asked where I lived. Then the cop who had stayed in the car looked at me closely and said, "Hey, you fit the description of the girl some grocery-store owner claims has been stealing from him. You know anything about a grocery store over on Maple Avenue?"

I vehemently denied any association and started crying again, telling them how worried I was because of the man who had been following me.

But I kept wondering—had I walked right into a trap? Was I making it easy for them to take me right down to the station and throw me into the slammer?

8

"What have you been doing this evening?" the first cop asked as we drove along—in the general direction of my apartment, I noticed.

Now I was trapped. What could I tell him?

"Oh, I was over helping to counsel some dope addicts."

"Helping drug addicts?"

"Yeah," I replied. "Somebody's got to do something to help these kids. They're dying of overdoses, working for pimps, and pushing the stuff. If somebody doesn't help them, they're all going to end up dead."

They both laughed at that. "Listen, there's no way anybody can help those junkies," one of them said. Then he asked, "Where do you meet with them?"

"Hey, I can't tell you that!" I countered. "You'd be over there to bust them, and you know that's not going to help them. They need someone who can understand where they're coming from. I used to smoke pot now and then myself. So I can help them."

Neither of them said anything about my answer. I don't know whether I convinced them or not. But when we drove by a corner where we were supposed to turn to go to the apartment, and they went straight, I asked, with fear rising in my voice, "Hey! Where are you guys taking me?"

"To jail."

I jumped forward and putting my hand on the shoulder of the cop driving the car said, "Hey, don't do that! I haven't done anything wrong! Since when is it a crime to be chased by a would-be rapist?"

"Oh, it's just that you fit the description we got on the radio," the driver said.

"Look, take me to my apartment," I begged. "My husband will verify where I've been tonight."

I knew Frank would cover for me—or at least I thought he would—if I could tell him first the lie I had told.

"You sure he can verify that?"

"You'd better believe it. In fact, he's a former drug user himself. He also belongs to this group. And furthermore, I'm really upset with you two. Here I'm trying to help junkies, and you're accusing me of being involved in some crime."

The driver laughed. "Take it easy, lady. We're not taking you to jail. We just thought we'd have a little fun."

"Fun? You're terrifying me half out of my skin!" I said, breathing a deep sigh of relief. And I decided I'd better keep my mouth shut the rest of the way home.

When they finally drove up into the parking lot of our apartment, I jumped out without even thanking them and ran inside.

Frank was pacing back and forth in the apartment

when I came in. He looked at me as though he'd seen a ghost and said, "Denise! Denise! How did you get away from those cops?"

"Well, I was waiting for you in that gas station when those turkeys drove up. They were checking with the mechanic, asking if he'd seen anything out of the ordinary. When they saw me, they started asking questions, and I had to make up a pack of lies. I told them that someone was following me, and I asked them to bring me home."

"You asked the cops to bring you home?"

"Sure. Why not? And when they asked what I had been doing, I told them that the two of us were working at a rehabilitation center for junkies. I told them you could verify that. I worried that maybe they'd get to you before I did, so when they drove up here, I just ran inside."

"Denise, you may think you're smart, but you're stupid!"

"Frank, don't say that to me!" I begged, flopping onto the sofa and starting to cry. "You don't know what I've been through tonight. If I hadn't talked my way out of things tonight, I could be sitting in the slammer right now!"

"Was one of those cops a really tall guy with a thin face?"

"Yeah, why?"

"Did you happen to hear his name?"

"Come to think of it, I did. Let's see—the mechanic called him Norman."

"Oh, no! That's Norman Lagevin. He's the smartest cop in this area. You are in trouble, Denise, big trouble!"

"What do you mean? I got here safe and sound, didn't I?"

"Yeah, you got here. But I don't know how safe and

sound. That Norman Lagevin outfoxed you. Now he knows right where you live. It's a trick he uses all the time."

"What are you talking about?"

"Well, one night I had burglarized a residence and was walking home. This cop stopped and offered me a ride. I was scared to death, wondering if he knew what I'd been up to. All that cop did—and it was that Norman Lagevin—was drive me home. I told him I'd been visting my girl friend in that part of town. He didn't say one thing about any robbery. But two nights later he appeared at my door and picked me up for questioning. How did he know where I lived? Because he had picked me up and had taken me home."

"But you didn't tell him anything then, did you?"

"Of course not. But he brought a couple of detectives with him, and they had a search warrant. They found some silverware I had stolen, so they took me down and booked me."

"Are you trying to say this cop is coming back later to get me?"

"You'd better believe it, Denise. You should have taken him to another place and then walked back here."

"But, Frank, I didn't think about that. Besides, I asked him to take me home. So how did he know I was involved in anything? The thing that worries me is whether or not that Shannon really did take some photographs."

"I've been thinking about that. I know that post office pretty well. I don't think he got pictures from inside it. The windows are situated in such a way that you cannot see inside the grocery store from over there. I think he's bluffing."

"Well, he also claimed that he got up over the walk-in cooler and was lying down up there, watching me."

"Did you go up there, Denise? Did you check the angle? Could he really see you from up there?"

"Well, I couldn't get up there then without his getting suspicious, so I really don't know."

"Don't you think you could have heard him crawling around back there if he had really done that?"

"Sure!" I responded. "If I had heard noises, I'd have gone back there to investigate, wondering if a burglar had sneaked in the back door."

"Then he's probably lying about the whole thing. He's got some suspicions, but there's no way he can prove anything. But if he's got evidence, you can be sure the cops are coming here!"

"You think I should have taken off?" I asked. "Does that make me look all the more guilty?"

"I don't know. But if the cops ask you about that, just tell them you were emotionally upset by his accusations—that no one had ever before accused you of being dishonest—and you just went to pieces."

I looked at my hands, trembling as though I were out in a snowstorm. "Frank, I've got to have something to calm my nerves," I said. "Have you got anything here?"

He smiled and replied, "Sure, baby. I've got something that will really cool your head."

He led me to the bathroom, reached up under the toilet tank, pulled out a stocking, and unfolded it. Oh, no! A hypodermic needle!

"Frank, no!" I protested weakly.

"Baby, this is where it's really at," Frank said soothingly. "Once you've done this, you can forget pot. This gives you a sensation you'll never believe. I know."

I started backing out of the bathroom, saying, "Frank, I just can't go that route. Pot's okay—but not heroin. I don't want to end up a junkie."

"Hey, what's to worry about?" Frank asked. "Just try

it this once. You'll get sensations you won't believe. I'm
not going to be a junkie. I can handle it. You can too.
But just try it once. If you don't like it, you can go back
to pot. No problem."

My hands were still trembling—both from the worry
that those cops might even now be building a case
against me and from what Frank was asking me to do.
But somehow his twisted logic made sense, and I said,
"Okay, I'll try it—but just once."

I couldn't believe this was really happening to me!
When he jabbed my vein, I had to look away because I
felt faint.

It all happened so quickly. He was right. I got a sensation I couldn't believe! It seemed as though every cell
in my body began to tingle. Then it felt as if I had shot
out of that apartment right into orbit. I didn't care about
anything or anyone.

Frank had shot the rest of the solution and was standing there smiling the biggest smile I'd ever seen.

We went out and sat on the sofa, our arms around
each other, rubbing and scratching. It felt absolutely
great.

The next thing I knew Frank was leading me to his
bedroom. But it didn't seem to matter now. Nothing
really mattered except feeling this way.

Later when I awakened, I realized I was in bed with
Frank. He was still asleep. So I slipped out of bed, feeling a little shaky but still kind of good. I knew one thing.
Heroin was indeed where it's at. I'd never fool with pot
again if I could get heroin!

Frank got up and dressed and told me he was hungry.
I fixed us roast beef sandwiches. As we sat at the kitchen
table eating, I asked, "Frank, what are we going to do
about the grocery store and the cops?"

"Maybe we'd better move," he said. "This place may
be getting too hot."

"Leave this beautiful apartment?" I moaned.

"Hey, don't worry about apartments. There are a lot more like this."

"But I like it here, Frank. I like being with you."

"Listen, baby, you get busted, and you won't be with me! So let's get out of here while we can. Besides, there's some other things I'd like to try. I've got a way of getting into the big time, baby!"

"What do you mean by that?"

"I can't tell you just now."

"Frank, you think Mr. Shannon's got evidence?"

He looked away from me. So I pressed him.

"Denise, I don't want to worry you," he said, "but the other day I ran into Pinky Samuelson. She used to work for Shannon. She's kind of cool and was ripping him off—like you were, I guess. He found out. Instead of calling the cops, he beat her up himself!"

"Oh? How bad? A couple of bruises?"

"Denise, I'm not trying to scare you, but Pinky had to go to the emergency ward at the hospital. He broke her arm, four ribs, blackened both eyes, and knocked out a couple of teeth."

"Frank, this is no time for that weird sense of humor of yours."

"Denise, I'm deadly serious. Old man Shannon is a sadistic maniac! I didn't know what I was getting you into!"

"Well, why didn't Pinky call the cops on him?"

"Ha! Since Pinky was stealing and Shannon knew it, how could she call the cops? She got what she deserved!"

His voice got deadly serious as he took my hand and said, "Denise, from what I understand, Shannon goes out and gets drunk and becomes a raging maniac. After that outburst last night, he's probably on a big drunk. Then he'll come looking for you."

"Well, he has no idea where I live," I said. "He didn't drive me home."

"What address did you put on that application when he hired you?"

Dumb me! I had put this address. Mr. Shannon would be able to come right to our apartment!

"What are we going to do, Frank? Call the cops?"

"Look, Denise, you know we can't call the cops."

I jumped up and threw my arms around his neck. "Frank, I'm scared. I'm really scared. Somebody is going to get me!"

"Well, I've got something for you. Something you may need."

He pulled a big switchblade out of his pocket and clicked it open. The thing looked a foot long. I pulled back in terror.

"What's that for?"

"You will be absolutely amazed at what this is for," he said. "At times this is better than a gun. Muggers use them. They come up behind a person and put a switchblade to his neck. If that happens to you, you're scared, really scared! That's why people give muggers everything they've got. Furthermore, if you get busted with a switchblade, it's not as bad as if you have a gun. You get busted with a gun, and you'll do a long time in the slammer. And these switchblades scare people to death!"

I looked at the one he was holding. It was scaring me to death just looking at it!

He held it out to me, and I said, "What am I supposed to do with that thing?"

"You are going to carry it from now on, baby. It's like an insurance policy—there when you need it."

I backed away, protesting, "Frank, I wouldn't know how to use one of those things."

"Listen, Denise, someday your life may depend on your being able to handle one. But most of the time it isn't like that. All you've got to do is show it, and it terrifies people into doing what you want them to do."

"What do you mean, show it? Should I stand there with it poised over my head?"

"No way, baby. You've got to be more subtle than that."

He placed the opened switchblade on the kitchen table, went to the closet, got my coat, and brought it to me. "Here, put this on," he ordered.

"Are we leaving now?" I asked, slipping the coat on.

"No, not yet. You've got to learn about the switchblade first. Now draw your arms up into the sleeves of the coat so your hands aren't visible. You know, like you do when you're really cold in the winter."

The coat was a little long, so I easily slipped my hands up inside of it.

He handed me the switchblade with, "Careful; it's sharp!"

Grabbing the right arm of my coat he said, "Now push that hand out. When I did, he laid the open switchblade on my hand. I started to shake.

"Now very gently grab the blade," he said. "That's right. Along your sleeve lengthwise. Good. Now draw your hand up inside your sleeve again."

As I did what he instructed, the knife disappeared from view.

"Now that's how you hide a switchblade," he said. "And if something comes up that you need to get it out of your hand quickly, just move your hand into your pocket. As you do, grab the handle of the switchblade, and click it shut. Nobody will know you have it. Only be careful; those things are razor sharp."

"Frank, why are we doing all this?"

"Well, I decided it's ridiculous for us to sit around and wait for Shannon to come looking for us. So we're going to go right to him. You are going back to that store with your hands drawn up in your sleeves, like you are now. Wait until no one else is around, and then go in and buy a pack of cigarettes. When Shannon is facing you, let your right hand drop down out of your sleeve so he can see that long switchblade. Then you tell Shannon that if he wants to try anything, to go ahead. But if he does, they are going to have to pick up the pieces of his body and glue them back together after you get through with him."

I was so startled by what Frank was suggesting that my hand flew open, and the switchblade clattered to the floor.

"Frank," I said, "you must think I'm absolutely stupid to try something like that! You told me that Shannon is a raving maniac. He'll grab that knife and cut me up!"

"Okay, Denise, go ahead and live in fear, if you want to. Every time you go out of this apartment, you'd better be on the lookout. Every time there's a knock on our door, you are going to wonder if it's old man Shannon. The only way to overcome your fears is to directly confront them."

"Frank, it won't work! I know it won't! I can't act and sound like a thug! It won't work!"

"It will work, baby! I know. You know Edie Wagner, the rich widow who lives in that big house by herself?"

"I've heard of her."

"Well, there were rumors around town that she had a lot of money and jewels at her place. One night I broke in, and she caught me with the stuff."

"No kidding!"

"Well, I had my switchblade with me, and I made a deal with her," Frank went on. "I had her gold necklace in my hand. I told her I'd give it back to her if she wouldn't call the cops on me. I also told her if she did call the cops, I'd be back and use my switchblade on her. I pulled this huge switchblade out, and you should have seen her eyes bug out! She was so scared she couldn't even talk. She just stammered. I knew I had her. To this day she hasn't called the cops. So, baby, I know it works!"

"But suppose old man Shannon's not afraid of switchblades. He's probably been threatened by all sorts of things in his store. Besides, he's not a little old lady."

"What I wish I had time to do, Denise, is to take you with me out on the street and let you watch me put this switchblade against somebody's throat." He picked it up from the floor and looked at it lovingly. "Baby, you'll never see anyone so scared in all your life."

Maybe Frank was right. He seemed to have been right about the problems we'd run into so far. Maybe I did have to confront Mr. Shannon to get over my fears. But what if I walked in there and showed him my switchblade, and he pulled a gun? A switchblade is no match for a gun!

"Come on, Denise; let's go over there right now," Frank said. "Let's get this over with. Besides, I can't wait to see Shannon's face when you confront him with that blade!"

As we drove all the way across town, I shivered with fright. What in the world was I getting into this time?

Frank stopped a block from the grocery store, pulled out that knife, opened it, and handed it to me. "All right now," he said. "Slip it up your sleeve just as I showed you. But be careful! It could slice your finger right off!"

I wished he'd quit reminding me of how sharp it was. That made me even more nervous. I placed the blade gently on my right hand and drew my arm up inside my coat. So far so good.

We drove up in front of the store and peered in. Sure enough, there was old man Shannon waiting on customers—three of them.

"Let's wait," Frank suggested.

After the customers left, Frank said. "Okay, Denise. Go get that guy. Grab him by the shirt and raise the switchblade to his neck if you have to!"

Still shaking, I stepped out of the car and walked into the store. Mr. Shannon was checking some bills and didn't look up until I walked to the counter and said, "I need a pack of cigarettes."

He immediately recognized my voice and screamed, "Get out of here now, Denise! Whether you know it or not, you are a marked woman. No one robs from me and gets away with it!"

"Mr. Shannon, look here."

Slowly I pushed my hand out of my sleeve, and more and more of the switchblade showed. His eyes started to bug out, and his mouth came open. It was like watching a movie in slow motion. Then he started backing up.

"Stay right where you are!" I ordered in my toughest voice. "I know all about you. I know what you did to Pinky Samuelson. Well, I just wanted to warn you. You try anything with me, and I'll kill you if I have to. This blade will slice you into little pieces so they can make sausage out of you. I know you think I took your money, but that's a lie. Now you stay away from me. You hear?"

Shannon's bottom lip started to quiver—like a little kid about to get a whipping. Frank was right. Shannon was absolutely terrified of a knife.

"You come after me, Mr. Shannon," I went on, "and I'm going to slice off all your fingers. Then I'll slash that ugly face of yours until even your own wife won't recognize you. Then I'm going to finish you off by putting this blade right through your heart. You're going to bleed like a stuck pig."

He had his hands up in the air, almost as though he was pleading for mercy.

"Do you read me, Mr. Shannon?"

He nodded vigorously, and I knew I had him. I slowly drew the switchblade up inside my sleeve again.

"Remember, Mr. Shannon, I don't expect to see you ever again," I said, backing toward the exit.

"It's too late, Denise," he called after me. "The cops already know about you. I told them where you live."

Oh, no! Then the cops really would be coming to our apartment! We had to get out of here.

I bolted for the car, yelling, "Frank, we've got to get out of here quick!"

He had kept the engine running, and the tires squealed as we took off.

"What's the rush, baby?" he asked. "I mean, you handled that like a pro all the way. I couldn't have done better myself. I could see out here how scared he was. Didn't I tell you that blade would scare the socks off of him?"

"Frank, it's not that!" I screamed. "Shannon said he's already called the cops on me and gave them my address!"

Even though we were already going too fast, Frank tromped down on the accelerator when I said something about the cops. He looked over at me, a frown creasing his face, and said, "Denise, we're in trouble. I mean, big trouble!"

9

As we sped back to the apartment, Frank kept repeating, "We're in trouble, baby, we're in trouble."

"How have things changed?" I asked.

"If Shannon has told the cops, they're going to come looking for you, Denise. And if they get a search warrant, then I'm in big trouble too."

"Frank, please don't talk that way! You're scaring me to death!"

"You're scared. I'm scared too! We've got to think of something quick!"

"Maybe we'd better not even go back to the apartment," I suggested.

"Are you crazy, woman? We have all that furniture and our clothes. I've got some drugs. Besides, my works are stashed there. We've got to have those works!"

Frank was driving too fast. Wouldn't it be ironic if the

cops pulled us over for speeding—and then discovered whom they had caught?

"Slow down!" I suggested.

When he didn't, I tried to reason with him. But he wouldn't listen. He was driving like a maniac. So it was with mixed emotions that I got out of the car when we screeched into the apartment parking lot. Would the cops already be here waiting for us?

Frank just sat behind the wheel of the car. "Aren't you coming in?" I asked.

"Baby, I've been thinking," he said. "We've got to move right now!"

"Right now? How in the world can we do that?"

"Don't ask questions!" he snapped. "Just get a move on. While you pack, I'll go get a truck. We'll load everything into that truck and take off now. It's the only way."

"Frank, do you know what you're saying? I can't just walk in there and throw everything into a suitcase. It'll take time to pack."

"We don't have time," he shouted angrily. "You take too much time, and we'll both be doing time. So just pack what you want. Don't worry about everything. If we don't get out of here right away, we're going to get busted."

"Where are you going to get a truck?" I asked.

"I noticed some U-Hauls at a gas station just down on the corner. I know the guy. I can work a deal."

Frank jumped out of the car and ran in the direction of the station without even saying good-bye. I hurried around back of the apartment complex, found some old boxes, and rushed with them to our apartment. Terrified because of the mess we were in, I started grabbing everything out of drawers and throwing it into the boxes. We had a couple of cheap suitcases, and I stuffed some clothes in them.

I hadn't gotten very far along before Frank came in and announced, "I got a good truck. Now we can get moving."

He enlisted a couple of fellows from down the hall. I've never seen people move as fast as they did. In less than two hours we had everything on that truck and ready to roll!

When I walked over to get into the truck cab. Frank asked, "Hey, what are you doing?"

"I'm getting into the truck. Aren't we ready to go? I figured if you thought enough of the furniture to take it, you'd also let me go along."

Frank pointed at his car and said, "Drive that."

"Frank, what are you talking about? I've never driven a car in my life!"

"Then it's time you learned. Everybody needs to know how to drive a car."

"Frank, you're crazy. I don't know the first thing about a car. I'd wreck it!"

By the way he gripped hard when he grabbed my arm, I knew he wasn't joking. "You're going to learn right now!" he announced.

"Frank, I can't! I can't!"

"Well, I'm not about to go off and leave my beautiful car," he said. "So you're going to have to drive it."

"But suppose I drive off the road and hit a telephone pole? Or run into somebody? Or go too fast?"

"Listen, Denise, driving is easy. All you need to do is follow the truck. I can't go too fast. So just follow me and stay alert. There's nothing to it."

He pushed me behind the steering wheel of his car and said, "Now listen carefully."

My knees were already shaking. If I had known this was going to happen, I would have practiced around the parking lot.

"Frank, I don't have a driver's license," I protested lamely.

"That doesn't surprise me," he said. "Someone who doesn't know how to drive usually doesn't possess a driver's license. So big deal. If a cop stops you, tell him it was stolen out of your purse at a dance last Saturday night. Make up something. But you're going to have to drive now!"

Argument apparently wasn't going to do any good. I'd better listen and learn all I could as fast as I could. But I just knew I was going to tear up his car and maybe get killed. Well, if I tore up his car, he'd probably kill me!

"You won't get angry with me if I don't do everything right, will you?"

"Will you shut up and listen?"

He pointed at the gearshift. "Notice that the lever is on P," he said. "That means 'park.' With this automatic transmission, there are two places on that shift where the car will start—P and N. Got that? Now when you put the key in the ignition, and the gearshift is in P, then you can turn the key, and the car will start. Understand?"

I nodded.

He handed me the keys. "Now start the engine."

My hands were trembling so that I couldn't even get the key into the ignition.

"For crying out loud, Denise, calm down. You're going to be all right!"

"Please don't yell at me, Frank."

"I'm sorry. Just put the key in. No, you've got it upside down. That's right. That way. Now slip it in there. Good. Now turn it away from you. That's right."

The whir of the engine coming to life told me I had done something right. But my heart was going faster than the engine.

"Now push down on the accelerator to get the feel of it."

I tromped down, and the engine raced like crazy.

"Not that hard! Not that hard!"

When I lifted my foot, the engine relaxed to a gentle purr.

"Just take it easy on the accelerator," Frank instructed. "You don't need to floor it. This thing's got enough power to leap tall buildings if you try something like that."

"Frank, I told you this would never work."

"Denise, it's got to work. Now listen closely. Notice those other letters on the gearshift. The R is for reverse and the D is for drive. All you have to do is to use those two. Now put your foot on the brake. Press down hard. And then bring the gearshift into reverse."

I yanked on it, but nothing happened.

"No, you'll have to lift up on it just a little," Frank said. "Then bring it down."

I followed his instructions and succeeded.

"Now put it in neutral," he said. And I managed to do that. Then he slipped behind the wheel, scooting me over a little. "I'll get you out of the parking lot," he said. "Then all you'll have to do is take a straight shot and follow me. Just keep it in drive all the way."

Frank whipped the car into reverse and had the thing out in the street in no time. Then he put it in neutral and told me all I had to do when he pulled out was to follow him, putting the gearshift in drive.

"That's all there is to it," he said, sliding out. "Put it in D, steer, and use the brake when you need to slow down. You don't need to shift when we stop for a traffic light or a stop sign. Just leave it in D."

"Frank, I'm terrified!"

He reached in and patted my hand. "Of course you're scared," he said. "So am I. But, baby, we're going to get out of this one. There are better things ahead!"

I was sitting behind the wheel now, and I noticed my

knuckles were white from gripping so hard. I watched Frank bring the truck around and start down the street, motioning for me to follow.

I jammed the gearshift into drive, hit the accelerator, and the car leaped forward, tires screeching. Terrified, I jammed on the brake. Then I hit the accelerator again.

Between my starting and slowing, Frank was getting ahead of me. I had to stay up with him. But I guess he must have been watching me in his rearview mirror because he slowed a little until I was right behind him.

After a few blocks my heart calmed a little. Maybe this wasn't going to be so bad after all. Fortunately there wasn't much traffic.

As I was rolling merrily along, I realized that I hadn't even asked Frank where we were going! I was so shook up over having to learn to drive that I completely forgot. Oh, well, I had to stay close to him anyway.

We headed north out of town. After we had driven for about an hour, he pulled to the side of the road, and I pulled behind him and stopped, pushing the gearshift into park. I let out another deep sigh. This wasn't all that bad. I guess I had thought driving was more difficult than it actually was.

When Frank jumped out of the truck and came back, he asked, "How are you doing?"

"Just fine. I was a little nervous the first few blocks, but I think I'm getting the hang of it."

He reached in and pinched my cheek lightly, saying, "You're all right, kid."

"Where are we going?" I asked.

"There are some motels up by the George Washington Bridge," he said. "We'll be there before long and can stay in one of them overnight. Then we can talk a little more about where we ought to go."

When Frank took off in the truck, I found it easier to follow him this time. I kept right behind him all the way until he turned off into a motel. I pulled alongside of him in the parking lot.

"Stay in the car," Frank said. "I'll go check on a room. I sure hope they aren't too much. I'm almost broke."

He seemed to take an eternity in the motel office. I looked around and wasn't too impressed with the place. But then, we'd only be here one night, so it wasn't a big deal.

When he didn't come and didn't come, I wondered if they were checking to see if we were married. No sense in worrying about that. Frank would think of something. He always did.

Finally he trudged out of the office and over to the car. "This place is a rip-off," he told me. "I had to work a deal with the guy, but we're in, baby."

"What kind of a deal?"

"No questions now. I'll tell you later."

Frank grabbed our suitcases out of the truck and we walked into room 102. "I miss our apartment already," I said, looking around at the sparsely furnished room.

"Hey, baby, this may not be as nice as our apartment, but it's better than some stinking jail cell! I'll bet the cops are there now, and old man Shannon is with them."

"You're probably right," I told him. "You usually are. But what's going to happen to us?"

"Well, we'll stay here tonight. Tomorrow we'll look for another apartment in the area."

I went over and flipped on the TV and sat on the edge of the bed. Frank came and sat beside me.

"Denise, I've got something to tell you," he said somewhat hesitantly.

"What, Frank?"

"We don't have any money. I don't have a dime on me."

"You don't have any money? How come?"

"I spent my last twenty bucks on a bag of dope."

"How much did you have to pay for this sleazy room?"

"It was free."

"Free? Come on, Frank. I'm not that naive. Nobody gets free motel rooms."

"Okay, Denise, it's kind of free."

"Stop talking in riddles! Either it's free or you pay for it. There's no in between. Now what's the deal?"

"I had to shoot the guy and steal the key."

"Frank, quit putting me on."

"I had to work a deal."

"Did you use your switchblade?"

"No, no switchblade."

"Come on, Frank, tell—"

Just then the phone interrupted our conversation, and I jumped sky high. "Who could that possibly be?" I asked nervously.

Frank walked over toward it, and I yelled, "Don't answer it! Maybe it's the cops! Maybe they trailed us here!"

"No," Frank said, almost offhandedly, "it's not the cops."

He answered and then listened for a moment. Finally he said, "I'm working on it. Just give me a couple of minutes more."

When Frank put down the receiver, I asked, "Who was that?"

"The guy who runs the motel."

"I thought you shot him."

"No, he's very much alive—and waiting for his end of the deal I made with him."

"Frank, this has gone on long enough. Now you tell me what kind of a deal you made."

"Just as I told you," Frank said, stalling, "I don't have a dime. I'm flat broke."

"You already said that."

"Well, when I went into the office, I knew I didn't have any money. I was figuring I could stall the guy by telling him I needed to make some phone calls and that I'd settle up the whole bill in the morning. I figured we could leave early in the morning and get the room free.

"Well, the guy told me a room would be fifty bucks."

"Fifty bucks for this fleabag?"

"I know it's outrageous," he responded, "but I wasn't planning to pay anything. So I said, 'Okay; I'll pay you in the morning.'

"The guy laughed and said, 'Do you take me for an imbecile? It's either cash or credit card—right now!'

"Well, I didn't have either, so I kept stalling, and the guy was getting madder and madder."

"Well, what did you do?" I interrupted. "Get to the point!"

"The guy watched us drive in, Denise. He saw you and asked if you were my wife, girl friend, or a girl from the street. I didn't know what to say, but I blurted out that you were my wife."

"Well, that makes me feel a little better," I teased.

"Well, then the guy looked at my hand and asked where was my wedding ring," Frank went on. "I stalled, and he said that the only way the two of us could stay in the same room would be if we produced a marriage certificate. I told him I lost it, and he started to scream at me to get out of his place. As I started toward the door, the guy called to me and said, 'I know that's not your wife. That's your girl friend. Right?'"

I stared at Frank. What was he leading up to?

"So I said to the guy, 'Suppose she's my girl friend?' And the guy tells me that he could work a deal with me."

"Frank, get to the point. I'm going to be an old woman before you finish this story!"

"Well, the guy asked if I wanted a free room and to

make some money besides," Frank went on. "I thought maybe he wanted me to do some work around here. But this is what he said."

Frank looked away from me.

"Go on! Go on!" I urged.

"The guy told me that we could have a free room if he could use my girl friend for just fifteen minutes."

"Are you driving at what I think you're driving at?"

"Listen, Denise, there's a guy in room one-ten who's looking for a good time with a girl. You go down there for fifteen minutes with that guy, and we've got a free room, and you can make a hundred bucks."

I stared at him unbelievingly for what he was asking me to do. "Frank," I finally said, "do you really want me to go down there and be a prostitute? You know I despise that. I would never, never, never, never in my whole life do something like that!"

"Denise, I guess I'm not painting the picture clear enough for you. We don't have any money. We've got to do something to get some. You want me to go out and mug somebody?"

"That's better than what you're asking me to do!"

"Okay, Denise, just forget it. I'll come up with something."

He winked at me and pulled two bags and his works out of his pocket. "Maybe this will help us figure a way out of this mess," he said.

We went into the bathroom and got off. I didn't know where Frank was getting his stuff, but it was fantastic. I went right into orbit.

Later when we were sitting on the bed, Frank put his arms around me and said, "Baby, we've got to make some money or we won't be able to get any more stuff."

Somehow nothing else seemed to matter, and I found myself saying, "Whatever you say, Frank."

"The guy is waiting in room one-ten," Frank said.

"Just think, baby—a hundred bucks and a free room."

I was so high I really didn't care what I did. I felt so good at that moment that I could face anything.

Frank picked up the phone, called the desk, and said, "She's ready." Then he walked over, kissed me, and said, "Baby, it's just for fifteen minutes. The guy at the desk told me the fellow is a salesman. He's not perverted, so you don't have to be afraid."

I really didn't want to go, but I was so high that I had no resistance.

As I started out the door, Frank said, "Don't forget your switchblade."

"You said the guy's okay. Why the switchblade?"

"Denise, you never know. Always take your switchblade."

When I found myself in front of room 110, I drew a deep breath and knocked. I heard someone moving inside; then the door opened. There stood a short, dumpy guy in his shorts and T-shirt. "Come on in," he said, looking me up and down.

He pointed to the bed, and I walked over. I wanted to make this quick and get out. It was quick. But it was also embarrassing and disgusting. I gathered up my things and headed back to our room, vowing I'd never do anything like it again.

"How did it go?" Frank asked when I returned.

I didn't answer. For one thing, I didn't know what to tell him. But I knew I'd never do it again.

Frank waved some money in front of my face and said, "Look, baby. A hundred bucks! You're okay!"

I walked into the bathroom, feeling as though I needed to vomit. I felt so dirty, so used.

Frank followed me in. "You'll never believe this," he said. "While you were gone, the guy at the desk called again. Another guy who just arrived also wants a girl. How about it?"

"Frank, please don't make me do that again!" I pleaded. "I'm just not up to it."

"Baby, it's a quick, easy way to get some money," Frank said, throwing his arms around me and hugging me. "And we're going to be needing a lot of money for an apartment and for dope."

I hugged Frank not because of what he was saying, but because in that moment I desperately needed his security and understanding. I had been through a traumatic experience. Surely he understood that.

He hugged me tighter, and then we kissed—a long one. Somehow I felt more secure in his love.

"Look what I found while you were gone!" he said.

I pushed back so I could see what he had in his hand—two more bags.

"Let's get off!" he suggested.

I wasn't about to argue. I needed to get high again to forget what I'd just been through.

After we got off and were sitting on the edge of the bed nodding and scratching, Frank said, "Baby, what do you think? I've worked a deal. This time we get a hundred and fifty bucks."

"What deal?"

"That other guy I told you about. I mean a hundred and fifty bucks for fifteen minutes isn't bad money!"

I didn't say anything, but I couldn't resist when Frank pulled me up from the bed, helped me into my coat, and headed me toward room 115. I was laughing now. I felt as though I could do this all night long. What did I care what happened, as long as I was high!

An extremely handsome man answered my knock at 115. I wondered why he wanted me. Wasn't he married? But I didn't ask questions. At this point I really didn't care.

When I got through and went back to our room. Frank met me with, "Baby, I just can't believe our good fortune! We came in here penniless, and now we've got two hundred and fifty bucks and a free room. Baby, you're priceless!"

I looked at Frank and asked, "Have you got any more dope?"

"No," he said, "but I've got money now. Let's go over the bridge into Manhattan. I know about a place down in the Lower East Side where we can get dope."

I didn't respond. At that point I was so totally worn out from all the experiences of the day and night that I flopped onto the bed and soon fell into an exhausted sleep.

The next thing I knew, the light of day was shining into our room. I had no idea of what time it was. I rolled over and realized Frank was still asleep.

I shook him and said, "Frank, what time is it?"

He rubbed his eyes, looked at his watch, and jumped up, saying, "It's almost noon!"

We ate a light breakfast at a nearby restaurant. Then Frank asked the guy at the motel if we could leave the truck parked on the lot while we went into Manhattan. The guy was all smiles as he said, "Why not?" He seemed to be glad to have me around!

When we got into the car and started toward the Lower East Side, Frank patted me on the knee. I wished I could have thought it was because he really loved me. But I was beginning to realize that he saw me as a source of financial gain—and what a horrible source! A prostitute! Was this what he had had in the back of his mind all the time?

We drove across the George Washington Bridge, down the FDR Drive, and onto Houston Street. A few blocks later we turned right, and I realized we were right in the middle of a place I had heard about but had never been to before—the Lower East Side.

Frank parked the car, and we looked around at the

burned-out buildings, the rotted and decaying tene-
ments, the filth and garbage everywhere. But the thing I
noticed most was the sad, sad people.

"Let's go down to that corner," Frank suggested.
"Someone there ought to be able to point us in the right
direction."

At the corner three junkies were leaning against a
building. Frank asked them. "Where can I get some
good dope?"

When the three guys looked me up and down, I realized I had no business being there. Now they figured we
had money, and they would mug us. And there was no
telling what they might do to me after that!

10

"Who are you?" one of the three junkies asked us.

"Hey, man, we're cool," Frank responded.

One of the junkies, sensing the possibility of some easy cash, started toward us. Frank sized up the situation instantly and whipped out his switchblade. "Like I told you, man, we're on your side," he said, brandishing his blade.

Taking the cue from Frank, I whipped out my switchblade, all the while glancing over to see what he was doing with his—then I did the same.

One of the junkies, noticing my obvious lack of experience with the switchblade, laughed and asked, "How many pigs have you stuck with that thing, girl?"

Thinking quickly, I responded, "I got a couple of tricks who tried to mess my body!"

"Okay," the junkie responded, "put those things away. You have nothing to worry about with us."

Frank didn't put his away, so neither did I.

"Like I said, man, where can I get some good dope?"

As if on cue, they all pointed down the street. One of them said, "See that guy over next to the phone booth? He's got it. And I mean, he's got good stuff."

"Thanks," Frank replied, and we backed away from them, putting our switchblades away when we had moved a little distance from them. I was learning to act tough, but I didn't know if I could ever cut someone with that knife.

Frank walked right up to the guy the junkies had pointed out and said, "I've got money; you've got some good dope?"

The guy eyed us suspiciously and asked, "Who sent you?"

Frank pointed to the junkies down the street. "One of those guys back there is a friend of mine," he said. "Me and my lady here are from Jersey. That guy said you had the best stuff on the Lower East Side."

"Yeah, I've got good stuff. How much do you need?"

"What's it selling for?"

"Twenty-five bucks a bag."

"I'll need eight bags."

"You say you're from Jersey?" the pusher asked.

"Yeah. Over across the bridge."

"You want to work a deal?"

"What kind of a deal?"

"I hear there are a lot of rich kids over in Jersey who are really buying. I've been thinking of trying to get a connection over there. Interested?"

"What's it worth to me?" Frank asked.

"I'll wholesale it to you in quantity for fifteen bucks a bag; you sell it for twenty-five. You make ten bucks a bag and get the stuff you use yourself wholesale. Okay?"

Frank glanced at me. When I nodded, he said, "Sounds like a good deal to me."

"Come with me," the pusher said.

We followed him down the street and walked up the stairs to the second floor of a dirty tenement. I thought I had been raised in poverty and filth, but this was another world to me. I couldn't believe the dirty graffiti all over the walls. And the stairwell stunk as though somebody—or somebodies—had been using it as a toilet! I couldn't imagine anyone living in filth like that!

We walked down a hallway, and the pusher knocked on a door. I noticed a strange peephole in the door covered by a little metal device. Evidently someone was behind it.

"How many bags now?" the pusher asked Frank.

"Thirteen," he answered.

I mentally calculated. Thirteen times fifteen would be $195. Frank would still have $55 dollars left from my last night's earnings. That would give us a little to eat and live on.

"Give me your money," the pusher ordered roughly.

Oh, no! Were we going to lose it all to a mugger here on the second floor of a dirty tenement?

Frank pulled out a wad of money—all my earnings—and counted out $195. The pusher took it and shoved it through the hole in the door, saying, "Thirteen bags."

While we waited, I studied our surroundings and became scared to death. This was a real hellhole. What in the world was a girl like me doing in a place like this?

In a few moments a brown bag was pushed through the hole in the door, and the guy took it and gave it to Frank. At least we had our dope. Now we had to get out of here.

"I'm usually out on the street," the pusher told us. "If you don't see me, ask around for Alonzo. Now get this straight. I don't carry dope on me—it's too dangerous. We always come up here to get the stuff. And let me warn you, before you get any ideas. This place is well fortified. If the cops come, we've got a foolproof escape route. And whatever you do, don't ever come here by yourself. Always contact me first, and I'll bring you."

"Sure, partner, anything you say," Frank responded.

"If you come by yourself, you might get shot," Alonzo went on. "These hallways have junkies all over. Some people get off down here. It's not safe for anyone. You hear me?"

Frank and I both nodded nervously. I knew that no way would I ever come here by myself. My life wouldn't be worth the snap of a finger!

"Now don't get greedy and shoot all that dope yourself," Alonzo warned. "Save yourself a couple of bags, sell the rest, and come back for more. The only reason I'm giving you that wholesale price is that I want to get in on that Jersey market."

"We'll be back," Frank responded. "You can count on us to build up your business."

At that moment I remembered how I used to feel about people who turned other people on to drugs—I thought they were the lowest of the low. But somehow now it didn't seem quite so bad. After all, we were getting our dope at a reduced price and were able to make money by selling it.

We walked down to the street with the pusher, back to our car, and took off again for New Jersey.

When we got back to the motel Frank told me, "What happened down there in the Lower East Side really opens a big door for us, Denise. I've been hoping to make a connection like that. It seems to me that we need to stay around here for a little while. Let me go talk to the motel manager and see if we can work a deal."

"Frank," I yelled as he started for the door, "I'm not about to go into those motel rooms like I did last night. I can't live like that!"

"Don't worry, baby," he said, coming back to give me a big hug. "Everything will be okay."

I flipped on the TV after Frank left, not at all convinced that everything would be okay. I knew Frank wouldn't hesitate to use my body if he had to.

When he came back, we both watched TV and then went out to get a little something to eat. We then cruised around until Frank spotted a pizza place where a lot of long-haired kids were hanging around. We parked, and he walked up to one of them and asked, "Want to buy some dope?"

"Hey, sure do!" one of the kids answered excitedly. "You know where we can get it?"

"Look, I've got the best stuff in America right here with me," Frank answered. "It's from Afghanistan. I mean, it's great stuff."

How did Frank know where it was from? Alonzo hadn't told us that. In fact, we hadn't gotten off yet ourselves so we didn't know if it was good or not. But I guess Frank was smart—selling some before we used any. If we started shooting, we might use up all thirteen bags!

"How much?" the kid asked.

"Just twenty-five bucks a bag—same price as on the streets of the Lower East Side," Frank said. "And you don't have the hassle of taking your life in your hands when you go down there. Want a couple of bags?"

"Sure do," the kid answered, "but I've got only twenty-five bucks on me."

"That's enough for one," Frank responded cheerfully.

The kid pulled twenty-five dollars out of his jeans and exchanged it for a bag of dope. Then he and a friend disappeared inside the pizza place, and other kids started coming out and buying. Before long Frank had sold ten bags—one hundred dollars profit.

"Let's get out of here," Frank told me.

When we got back to the motel, we got off. It was good stuff. But no sooner was I high than Frank said, "How about it? Ready to make some more money for us?"

Dope melted my resistance; I just didn't care what I did. That night I had two more men at a hundred dollars each. At least the money was good, but I still felt cheap and dirty after each encounter.

About two in the morning Frank walked into our motel room, carrying our stereo. "I know where I can get fifty bucks for this from a fence in town," he announced proudly.

"Frank," I protested, "that's our stereo. I enjoy it."

"Come on, don't hang onto things like that," he chided. "Everything's got its price. You've got to move things while you've got the chance. That fifty bucks will buy three bags of dope. Look at it as an investment. We get the money, buy dope, sell it at a profit, and buy more dope to sell. Pretty soon we'll be able to buy this motel. I'll be a big businessman!"

I realized I was getting in deeper and deeper into illegal activities—and demoralizing activities. Where would it all end?

"Listen, baby," Frank went on, "I've worked with fences before when I burglarized houses. I know I can get good money for this stereo. And I got such a good deal when I bought all that furniture that you might say we got the stereo free. That means I'll be making fifty bucks clear profit on the deal!"

I couldn't quite follow Frank's twisted logic, but I realized there was no sense in arguing with him. So we got into the car, drove into town, and finally spotted some guys who were high. Frank got out of the car and talked to them. They pointed down the street.

We drove to where they had pointed. Frank walked in

with the stereo while I waited in the car, and in a few minutes he came back—without the stereo.

"I got fifty bucks," he said.

I guess he knew I was upset with him because as soon as we got back to the motel, he suggested we get off again. As soon as I got high, everything seemed so mellow and peaceful. Nothing bothered me.

The next day started the pattern all over again—back to the Lower East Side to buy more dope, sell it to the kids that night, then go back to the Lower East Side again the next day. We were getting pretty well acquainted with Alonzo by then, and he seemed happy with all the new business we were getting for him.

The only thing different from the first night was that during the next three weeks or so Frank didn't make me go to bed with any more johns. I guess he was making enough money pushing drugs that he was satisfied.

One day Frank worked a deal and sold all the furniture in the truck. That really disgusted me. I wondered if we'd ever get another beautiful apartment like the one we'd had. Besides, I hated living in this sleazy motel.

Frank and I were using more and more of the dope ourselves. We sort of gradually worked into it and hardly realized what was going on. I think one thing that happened was that the manager of the motel really wanted my services for the men who stopped there, and he talked Frank into using me for prostitution. I still didn't like it, but Frank would get me high and then suggest that there was someone waiting for me in one of the rooms. When I was high, I had no willpower, no ability to resist his suggestions.

In my lucid moments I wondered where it would all end. Frank kept getting more and more customers, and with that much dope coming in, the cops were sure to get suspicious. Since we were going into the Lower East Side almost every day, they might readily suspect us.

And if they heard there was a prostitute residing at our motel, they might just set up a trap for me. It was dreadful living in fear on the wrong side of the law. But whenever I shot up some dope, suddenly nothing really seemed to matter at all.

One morning I woke up and realized I was getting sick. I knew what was happening. My body was now demanding dope. I was hooked! And unless I got some dope right away, I'd start into withdrawal—with nausea, cramps, profuse sweating, and hell on earth!

Frank was already up and lolling in a chair. "Hey, I need some dope right away," I said. "I'm getting sick."

"Sorry, baby," Frank responded. "I don't have any. I had a good night last night and sold it all."

"Then let's go right away and get some more," I said. "If I don't get some, I'm going to puke."

"You've been around too many junkies and heard them talk," Frank said patronizingly. "That kind of nonsense is all in your head. You can wait."

I noticed Frank was kind of nodding. Then I looked closer and realized the pupils of his eyes were pinpointed. "Frank, did you just get off?" I demanded.

He laughed and said, "Yeah, baby, about an hour ago. I tried to wake you up, but you were really sawing logs, so I got off by myself."

"That's a lie!" I shouted, leaping toward him and shaking him. "You know I would have gladly gotten up and got off with you!"

He was still laughing as he said, "I tried, baby; I tried!"

"Come on, Frank," I said, trying to pull him out of the chair. "We've got to go get some more dope now. I'll forgive you for not waking me if we can go get some now. Man, I'm sick!"

"Get your own money for dope," Frank sneered. "Why should I have to supply you all the time? Just go knock on some of those motel doors, get a trick, and earn some money. Then we'll talk about it."

Enraged, I started pounding my fists against his chest, cursing him and shouting, "Frank, you come with me to that car before I pull my switchblade on you!"

He laughed and slid out of the chair onto the floor. I grabbed my switchblade off of the nightstand, flipped it open, and stood over him.

He looked up at me blankly and said, "Hey, baby, cool it, will you? You really look mean with that thing!" Then he giggled.

Moving the blade closer to him, I shouted, "I'm ready to puke, and if you don't get up, I'll puke all over you! Now get up off that floor and let's get going!"

Frank got up unsteadily and started weaving across the room. I wondered how many bags he had loaded into the cooker this time. He had started using two every time he got off now. Maybe he had tried three. We were both noticing that it took more dope each time for us to get that high feeling.

Frank staggered to the dresser, picked up his keys, and threw them at me with, "Here, baby; go get your own dope."

"Frank, be serious!" I pleaded. "I don't have a driver's license. And I sure don't want to have to drive in that New York City traffic."

"Baby, let me tell you something." Frank's words slurred as he moved unsteadily toward me. "I couldn't drive if my life depended on it. I'd be all over the road, and a cop would bust me before we ever got to the Lower East Side. And I don't have any desire to get busted. Now if you'll wait until this afternoon, maybe by then I'll be able to drive. . . ."

I picked up the keys from where they had fallen on the floor. I couldn't wait until afternoon. I had to have dope and have it now!

As if to confirm that diagnosis, my stomach tightened, and I headed for the bathroom. The vomit splattered all over the toilet. So this was where it all ended. I was hooked, and I had to have dope—at any price, at any sacrifice. And I was beginning to realize I was going to have to have more and more and more.

I came out of the bathroom moaning, "Frank, I'm sick; I think I'm going to die!"

Seeing my obvious distress frightened him, and he peeled off two twenties. "Here's some money for your dope," he said. "That'll get you two bags with some extra for gas or something if you need it. And tell Alonzo I'll be down later on today."

I snatched the money he held out, finished dressing, and headed for the car.

I put in the key and turned it. The engine ground and ground and finally whirred to life. So far so good. I gently backed out, eased onto the main highway, and started for the city. Fortunately, I had helped Frank watch the street signs when we had gone down there each day, so by this time I knew the way quite well, and I made it down to the Lower East Side without incident—except that my stomach was still churning.

At our usual place I pulled to the curb and started looking for Alonzo. I guess I must have gotten there earlier than we usually did because I couldn't find him anywhere—just my dratted luck.

My stomach tightened again with severe pain—as though a switchblade were jamming into it. The vomit splattered all over the sidewalk and even onto my feet, but I didn't care. Nothing mattered now but finding Alonzo and getting some dope so I could get off.

Spotting a junkie leaning against a building, I said, "Hey, where can I get my dope? I need some dope!"

He laughed. "If you find some, baby, give me some too. I need some too!"

That greedy junkie—he looked as though he had just gotten off!

I walked the other direction. Where was Alonzo? I stood next to the phone booth where we usually met him and waited. He was always here. Where was he now that I needed him so desperately? Maybe it was too early. I'd have to go up there myself!

Finding the dirty tenement wasn't difficult. We'd been there every day for several months now. I nervously walked up the filthy stairs to the second floor, down the hallway to that special door. Holding my breath, I knocked. No answer! I knocked harder. Still no response. So I opened up the peephole and stared into an eye looking out at me. Frightened, I jumped back.

Some guy yelled, "Hey, kid, what are you doing here?"

No sense beating around the bush in an emergency like this, I told myself. So I said, "Man, I need three bags quick! I'm puking all over the place!"

"Hey, I recognize you," the guy said. "You're one of Alonzo's Jersey connections, aren't you? You come up here regularly."

"Yeah, that's me. My man usually handles the transactions, but he couldn't come this morning. Here's forty bucks. Can I have three bags? We'll pay you the extra five dollars the next time we come. I think Frank plans to come this afternoon. Okay?"

"Not so fast, girl. The stuff is twenty-five dollars a bag."

"But you always sell it to us for fifteen!" I wailed.

"That's wholesale. You've got to buy in quantity to get that price. You buy a couple of bags, and it's twenty-five bucks a bag, or no deal."

My stomach tightened again, and I doubled over with pain.

"Okay, have it your way," I said in disgust. "Give me a bag. But, man, I've got to get off now!"

I shoved my forty dollars at him and in moments the guy pushed a little bag through the hole in the door. Inside was my bag and fifteen dollars change. Finally!

I knew I could never make it back to the motel without getting deathly ill. I had to get off now. So I knocked on the door again. The little peephole opened, and the guy asked, "Now what?"

"Have you got a set of works?" I asked. "I've got to get off now. I'm puking all over the place."

"Go up to the next floor. At the end of the hall Tony has a set of works. But he'll want a taste before he lets you use them."

I knew what that meant. He wanted some of my dope. But at least I'd still have enough to get straight and get over this pain and sickness.

"Thanks," I said.

"Listen, kid, be careful, will you? This tenement has junkies all over the place; muggers too. It doesn't make any difference to them who they mug. So be careful. You hear footsteps behind you, and you run for your life!"

I should have listened carefully to his warning. But at that moment I didn't care about junkies; I didn't care about muggers; I didn't care about anything. The only thing I wanted—and had to have—was to get off.

I ran up the stairs, down to the end of the hall, and knocked on the door. When no one answered, I kicked on it in desperation. Finally it opened slightly.

"The guy downstairs sent me," I explained. "I understand I can use your works."

He unlatched the chain and invited me in. He looked me up and down—like those filthy johns did. It made shivers run down my spine. What was I doing in a place like this all by myself?

"My home is your home, baby," he said cordially.

No sooner was I inside than I doubled up from the pain in my stomach. The guy gently put his arm around me and said, "Easy now, kid; everything's going to be all right. Easy now."

I handed him my bag, and he grabbed it and headed for his bathroom. When he finally came out, I looked at the needle. The greedy bum had used half of it! But I was too sick to care.

"Here, let me help you," he offered. He wrapped the stocking around my arm, and I pumped up my veins. The dope hit, and the pain went away.

I drew a deep breath, already feeling much better. I knew I wouldn't get high on this—I was too hooked for that. But at least I could get straight and drive back to the motel. Maybe by now Frank would be ready to come back with me and buy some more dope.

As I started to leave the apartment, Tony said, "Baby, I kind of like you. You looking for some guy to take care of you?"

"Listen, I've got my own man," I answered. "Besides, I'm not a prostitute, and I can't stand pimps!"

Tony grabbed my arm and said, "Kid, I don't know who you are or what you're doing down here, but you're way out of your element. You'd better get out of this place quickly. There are all kinds of people in this tenement—junkies, perverts, muggers, you name it. An attractive young girl like you is fair game for anything—including rape!"

I guess he must have seen the terror in my eyes when he mentioned rape for he quickly reassured me, "No! No! I'm not going to try anything! I'm just warning you to get out of this place now! You have no business being here by yourself!"

Terrified now, I ran out of his room, down the hallway, and started down the steps. I hadn't gotten down more than four steps when I felt a hand grab me and then the cold steel of a switchblade press against my neck.

I started to yell, but a big hand slapped over my mouth, and a guttural voice intoned, "Girl, you yell, and I'm going to jerk this switchblade right through your throat!"

My heart was beating like crazy. What did he want? My money? My body? Both?

I tried to turn around to face him, but I couldn't move. He pulled his hand away from my mouth and started running it all over my body. In frustration he growled, "Where do you keep your money, girl?"

I had put the fifteen dollars in a pocket in my sweater, but I wasn't about to tell him.

His hand was searching every square inch of my body. "Okay, girl, where's the money? Where's the dope?"

"I've already shot up the dope," I said.

Then his hand ran into my sweater pocket and pulled out the fifteen dollars. The next thing I felt was a strong shove, and I went hurling down those stairs. I hit the bottom on my right shoulder, and the pain was so excruciating that I thought I must have broken something. I slowly got up, holding my shoulder because of the terrible pain, and looked back up the stairs. Nobody in sight. Whoever mugged me probably had gone down the fire escape or maybe into one of the apartments.

I was furious! If I ever got near that guy, I would kill him. I didn't get a chance to see what he looked like, but I was sure I'd recognize that voice again. I reached for my switchblade, deciding to keep it handy if I had more trouble before I got to the car. My switchblade! It wasn't there! He must have lifted that too!

I limped down the rest of the stairs to the street, wondering what I should do. Should I call the police and report it? Or should I just go back to the motel? Would the police even bother with a mugging of fifteen bucks?

My mind was befuddled. I decided that what I needed to do was to call Frank. He would have an idea of what I should do. I always counted on Frank to make decisions like this for me.

But how was I going to call Frank? I didn't have any money, and it would be at least seventy-five cents to call over there.

As I walked toward the car, trying to figure out how I was going to get some money, I spotted Alonzo standing on the corner. Just my luck—to find the pusher now that I didn't need him. But wait! He'd spot me the change for a phone call to Frank.

"Hey, Alonzo," I called. "I need seventy-five cents."

He stared at me. "What in the world are you doing here, girl? You must be crazy to come here. Where's your old man?"

"He's sick," I lied. "But he'll be down this afternoon. He said for me to tell you that."

"How many bags you want now?"

"Hey, I forgot to ask Frank," I lied. "I need that seventy-five cents to call and ask him."

"You came all the way down here and didn't ask him how many bags? You're stupid, kid."

"I guess you're right. I was so nervous that I just forgot. But have you got three quarters I can borrow? I've got to call Frank and find out what I should do."

Alonzo pulled out some change and handed it to me. I grabbed it and ran to the corner phone booth.

Just before I got there I passed a couple of guys. I don't know what made me do it—being nervous I guess—but I asked them, "Hey, have you got a cigarette?"

They stopped and looked me up and down in a way

that really made me nervous. Why had I done something so stupid as this?

Finally one of them pulled out a pack, shook out a cigarette, and handed it to me.

"You got a match?" I asked, sticking the cigarette in my mouth.

One guy pulled out a lighter, flipped it, and held it to the cigarette. In the same instant the other one whipped out his switchblade and held it to my throat.

"Come with us!" he ordered. "One yell, and you're dead!"

My knees buckled, and I felt as though I was going to faint on the spot. But the two of them grabbed me and headed down the street a few steps to where they pushed me inside a deserted tenement. Then both of them started to laugh fiendishly. Were these two maniacs going to kill me?

11

When I started to scream, one of the guys whipped out his switchblade, jammed it in my ribs, and threatened, "Kid, one more scream out of you, and I'm going to slash your guts open!"

I knew these were no ordinary muggers, and when they started dragging me down the deserted hallway, I instinctively knew what they had in mind—rape!

There wasn't a person left in this burned-out tenement. What good would it do to scream? I'd just keep my wits about me, and maybe I could get away in an unguarded moment.

At the end of the hallway they forced me into a room and shoved me to the floor. As I hit the floor, I rolled over to jump up and run for the knocked-out window. I didn't know where it went to, but anywhere was better than with these two thugs!

Just as I thought I might get away, one of them leaped

after me and just barely grabbed my hair—but it was enough to jerk me back and pull me off my feet onto the floor again.

Squirming and yelling, I tried my best to fight them off. That's when one of them put his switchblade against my neck and clapped his hand over my mouth. I knew then that to continue to resist meant almost certain death.

It was unbearable, and I wanted to scream. In my mind I did scream. I cried out to God to help me, to spare my life from these two maniacs. They were worse than animals!

Afterward, one of them said, "You go to the cops, kid, and we're coming back to kill you!"

I didn't respond. I couldn't respond. But I was looking, getting their features clear in my mind. One of them was dark with a moustache; the other had a round face, no moustache. I would never forget those two faces!

When they walked out, I lay there too stunned and too aching to move a muscle. Later when I was able to sit up, sharp, stabbing pains accompanied every little move I made.

I finally was able to crawl around the room and retrieve my clothing. I got dressed and then stumbled along the hallway back to the street. Every step was pure torture.

When I got to the street, I cautiously looked around. The two guys were nowhere in sight.

Now I was really in a dilemma. I didn't know if I should call the cops on that mugger. Should I call them to report a rape? Or were those two goons serious in their threat to kill me if I reported them?

I didn't know what to do, so I figured I'd better do what I was starting to do when they forced me to go with them: I'd better call Frank.

The phone booth was just a few steps away. I reached into my jeans and pulled out the change Alonzo had given me. At least those monsters hadn't ripped off my money.

When I got Frank on the phone, I yelled, "Frank, I've been raped by two maniacs!"

Silence.

I yelled it again: "Frank, I've been raped!"

He let out a torrent of curses such as I had never heard from him before. Then the threats came: "I'll kill them! I'll kill them!"

"Frank, calm down. What should I do? Should I call the cops?"

"No, don't call the cops, Denise. When I get through with those guys, they're going to need an undertaker. Nobody is going to touch you and get away with it!"

"But, Frank, what should I do? Should I stay here? Should I drive back to the motel?"

"Where are you now?"

"I'm on East Sixth, at the telephone booth where we make connection with Alonzo."

"Stay right there. I'm coming right now."

I started to say something else, but Frank had hung up. Now I really was worried. Would I be an accomplice to a murder? Wouldn't it be better to turn the matter over to the cops? Besides, those two maniacs were vicious. How would Frank be any match for the two of them?

But although I was worried about the whole situation, I felt better knowing that Frank was coming. I always felt safer with him around.

I walked back to the corner, shifting my weight from one foot to the other to try to ease the pain. I was hoping against hope that Frank would get here quickly, because if somebody else grabbed me, I'd be a goner.

Alonzo walked up and asked, "You and your old man get into a fight?"

Should I tell him what happened?

"Hey, you even got your blouse torn," he went on. "Somebody really must have wanted whatever it was you had."

"That's not funny, Alonzo. I was just raped."

"Listen, I told you you were stupid for coming down here. Any girl like you, coming to a place like this, has to be out of her mind. You're lucky you're still alive. Every day the cops find girls like you dead in the alleys." He pointed his finger at me to emphasize it: "I told you you had no business coming here. You deserve what you got!"

Raging at his impertinence and total lack of sympathy for my suffering, I raised my hand to smack his face. He jumped back cagily with, "Hey, cool it, before *I* try something!"

I dropped my hand to my side, terrified. I knew I'd be no match for his brute strength.

"Well, why don't you just stick around, Alonzo? You're going to see what happens when somebody rapes me. Frank is on his way down here now. He's going to kill those guys!"

"Hey, this is going to be interesting. I'm in the mood to see a good fight. What did the guy who raped you look like?"

"There were two of them."

"Two?"

"Yeah. One had a moustache; he was kind of small and dark. The other had a round face, no moustache. I guess they were both about five-foot-six."

"Oh, oh," Alonzo said. "I think I know who those two guys are. And you weren't their first victim. You ran into a couple of the meanest dudes alive, known as Flip and Chuck."

"You know them?"

"Well, Denise, the Lower East Side has its own rules

of survival. Just about everybody down here is either on drugs or is pushing drugs. Nobody is safe. But there are certain characters who specialize in certain things. Flip and Chuck—their specialty is rape. Every so often some stupid girl like you comes down here by herself, and Flip and Chuck do their thing. I don't know how many women they've raped, but they brag about it."

"Well, their bragging is about to come to an end," I predicted. "Frank said he was going to kill them both. So I'll be the last one they ever rape."

Alonzo laughed. "You kids sure have a lot to learn," he said. "You should have seen what happened to the last guy who tried to do them in. They found his body in back of that tenement over there." He pointed down the street.

"Flip and Chuck really went berserk on that character. They must have pumped fifty bullets into his body!"

Was Alonzo telling the truth? I looked again at where he had pointed, and whom should I see but those two rapists!

I nodded in their direction and whispered, "Alonzo. Look over there. That's the two!"

"Yeah, that's Flip and Chuck all right," Alonzo answered. "Let me tell you, Denise, those two are fearless. When Frank comes around, you'd better make up some big lie. If you put the finger on Flip and Chuck, you might as well kiss Frank good-bye."

"Why are telling me this?"

"For selfish reasons. I think I can trust you and Frank with the drugs I sell. You've built up a good trade for me, and I don't want to lose one of my dealers."

"Thanks a lot, buddy," I said sarcastically.

"Well, I have to keep an eye on my business. And speaking of business, I have some to attend to right now. You stay here and wait for Frank, but keep your eyes on those two characters."

I grabbed his sleeve and pleaded, "Please don't leave me, Alonzo. Those two animals might try it again!"

"It's possible," Alonzo replied. "They stop at nothing."

Throwing my arms around him, I begged, "Please don't leave me!"

"Okay, you and Frank have been good customers. I'll stay with you until he gets here. But you've got to promise me not to put your finger on Flip and Chuck. Those two are maniacs."

"Okay, I'll think of something," I promised. "But please don't leave me."

"Let's go get a cup of coffee," he suggested. "You look as though you could use something. And they won't bother us in the coffee shop."

What I really needed was to get off. But I didn't have any money for that now. Maybe Frank would bring some money with him.

In the coffee shop, when I picked up the cup, my hands trembled so that I could hardly bring the cup to my lips. Alonzo reached across the table and steadied my hand. "Don't take it so hard, baby. It happens all the time. And you're lucky to still be alive!"

I was alive all right, but something had happened to me emotionally. I was ready to kill those two maniacs myself—to tear them limb from limb. But I knew I had to restrain myself for Frank's sake. I didn't want his blood all over the street.

About forty-five minutes later I saw Frank out on the sidewalk. Alonzo ran out and hailed him, and I hobbled out to the street. As soon as Frank saw me, he ran up and threw his arms around me. "Baby, are you all right?" he asked consolingly. Then as his conscience struck him he muttered, "I never should have made you come down here by yourself. I'm sorry. I didn't know what I was doing."

"It's okay, Frank. I'll be all right. I'm a little sore, but I'm still alive. Let's just get some dope and go back to the motel."

"We'll do that, Denise. But I've got some other business I've got to take care of first."

"Frank, you're no match for them."

"That's what you think, Denise. Look here."

He pulled his hand out of his pocket, and there was a gun!

"Where did you get that?" I asked in astonishment.

"I bought it a few days ago. I decided I needed better protection. I didn't tell you because I thought it might scare you. But I'm going to use it to finish off those monsters."

Across the street Flip and Chuck were pointing over our way and laughing. I almost said, "That's them, Frank." But I knew if I did, there would be a shoot-out.

"I really couldn't tell what they looked like," I said lamely.

"But, Denise, it's broad daylight!"

"But they took me into a burned-out tenement."

"Well, maybe if we drive around, you'll see them and recognize them. The motel manager let me borrow his car, so we can use it. Can you give me any kind of a description?"

To try to save Frank's life I said, "Well, one guy had red hair and must have been at least six feet tall—skinny too. The other one was blond and even taller."

"Are you sure?"

"Of course I'm sure of that much."

"Denise, I've never seen any tall guy with red hair around here."

"Well, maybe they're just new in town. Besides, I think I went into shock. You know how people sometimes appear bigger than they really are when they're about to hurt you."

"Well, let's look," Frank said. "If you spot them, just point them out and leave the rest to me."

Frank drove slowly down one street and up another. Whenever he saw two guys together, he would ask, "Is that them?" Once he actually pointed to Flip and Chuck and asked the question. Deep within I wanted to say that it was; I wanted to see those goons get what was coming to them. But I knew they would get Frank—and maybe me too. I couldn't take that chance.

We must have circled for at least two hours, with Frank getting more and more into a wild rage. It's a good thing I didn't point out anybody because he would have jumped out of the car and started pumping bullets into them without asking any questions.

When it became apparent that the search was futile, Frank said, "Well, let's get some dope and get back to the motel. But every time we come here, I'm going to plan on spending a couple of extra hours, looking for those goons."

We got our dope without further incident, and Frank drove me back to where I had parked his car. As I started to pull from the curb, he honked, got out of the car, and walked back to me.

"I don't want to scare you, Denise," he said, "but I'm going to take a different route back to the motel."

"Why?"

"Oh, it's nothing. But we'll go through the Lincoln Tunnel and up that way."

When Frank started to pull his head out of the opened window, I grabbed him and demanded, "What's the matter?"

"Nothing, Denise. I just like to be cautious in this business. Now you just follow me, and everything is going to be all right."

I didn't like what he said or the way he said it, so I demanded again, "Tell me what's the matter!"

"Hey, I may just be paranoid. It's nothing."

"But why are we going back another way?"

"Because I think someone has been following me."

"Following you? Why?"

"Don't be stupid, Denise. The other night on the street I heard that the cops were starting a crackdown. They know there's more dope coming in. They say they are even following people into New York. So the cops could be after us."

"Are you sure, Frank?"

"No, I'm not sure. I may be paranoid. But I don't want to take any chances. When we head back, we'll pick different directions. Then if we're being followed, either we'll be able to tell it or maybe they'll just lose us."

As Frank walked back to the motel manager's car, I started trembling all over again. Were the police really onto us? If they busted us with that dope Frank just bought, it would be all over for us!

I followed Frank to the Lincoln Tunnel without any difficulty. I was even getting used to driving in heavy traffic. But in the tunnel we hit a traffic jam and just barely inched forward.

That traffic jam gave me time to reflect on my life. How had I ever gotten into such a terrible mess? I was raped. I was racked with pain. I was hooked on drugs, living with a pusher, and prostituting to support our habits. I was doing all the things I had said I never would do under any circumstances. What on earth had happened to me?

As I sat there thinking, all of a sudden I seemed to be thrown into the very pit of hell. I kept getting raped over and over and over. Then I was screaming, totally out of control of my emotions. I couldn't go forward, so I jammed the gearshift into reverse, tromped on the accelerator as hard as I could, and felt the car fly backward. I heard metal crunch and break.

The next thing I remember was raising my head up in an ambulance and hearing the siren screaming. An attendant was bending over me, and I asked, "What happened?"

"You got yourself into a little accident."

"How? What? Where?"

"Don't ask me," he replied. "All I do is pick up the pieces. I don't fill out accident reports."

"Where am I going?"

"To a hospital, of course. You've been banged up a little."

I poked around on my body and couldn't feel any place that hurt—except I was still in pain from the rape.

"I think I'm okay," I announced.

"Listen, lady, you're not okay. They had you handcuffed when we picked you up. You were screaming obscenities and were out of your mind. We are taking you to Bellevue Hospital."

"Hey, stop this rig right now and let me out. I'm okay, and I'm sure not going to Bellevue. You think I'm nuts?"

"Lady, I told you all I do is pick up the pieces. When we get to the hospital, a doctor will check you over. He'll decide whether you're all right or not. Now the cops told us to take you to Bellevue, and that's exactly what we're going to do."

I started to sit up and realized I was strapped down. My legs were strapped down too. Did they think I was insane?

At Bellevue they whisked me into the emergency room. The doctor looked me over and asked, "What's the matter with you?"

"Doc, there's nothing wrong with me. It's all a big mistake. Now unstrap me and let me go."

The doctor looked down and smiled knowingly. I started screaming and cursing—him, the hospital, the nurses. That's when he motioned for two attendants to take me. They pushed me down the hall and into an elevator and started up. I realized then that they weren't going to let me go. Maybe I should have controlled my temper a little more in that emergency room.

They took me to an upstairs room, and there a nurse hit me with a needle. I felt myself going.

When I awakened later, I struggled until I realized I was still strapped down. Then a nurse came by and in a syrupy-sweet voice asked, "And how are we doing?"

"What do you mean?" I yelled at her. "You're doing okay, but they've got me strapped down where I can't even move. Let me go!"

"Temper, temper!" she said sweetly. "Don't take it so hard. We really aren't all that bad in here."

"Am I in a nuthouse?" I asked.

She laughed. "Of course not. This is a hospital. We serve the needs of the city."

"Is this Bellevue Hospital?"

She nodded.

"Isn't this where they take the criminally insane?"

She nodded again. "Yes, we do have a ward for them."

"What ward am I on?" I pressed.

"You are in the drug detoxification unit."

"Detoxification?" I yelled. "I'm no junkie."

"Then what are those marks on your arms?"

"Scratch marks. I was raped today."

"Well, we know you were raped. The doctor's medical examination showed that."

"Medical examination? That doctor in emergency hardly even looked at me."

"The doctor examined you while you were out, deary."

"Hey, that's dirty pool."

"Well, the examination also showed you've been on

drugs. We'll give you some methadone to bring you down."

When she turned to walk away, I yelled, "Take these straps off me right now. I demand that you do it!"

The nurse called back, "Things will go a lot better if you cooperate with us. Don't make it hard on yourself."

"Look, I didn't ask to be brought here. I told the ambulance attendant I didn't want to come here. So I'm here against my will. I'm going to have my lawyer sue all of you. Let me out now, and I'll call it off."

"I'm sorry," she replied. "I don't have the authority to take off those straps even if I wanted to. Only the doctor can decide that. Since you're going to have to stay here, you might as well make the best of it."

I struggled vainly against those straps, but they held me fast. Then the nurse disappeared down the hall. Somehow I had to get out. Somehow I had to escape. And then an idea began to form in my mind.

Later that afternoon the nurse came back with a dose of methadone. When she hit me with it, I immediately felt better.

"Do you want to be a hero?" I asked her.

She looked at me, smiled, and answered simply, "No."

Since that approach wasn't working, I tried another.

"You believe in law and justice, don't you?"

"Well, if you're talking about punishing people who commit crimes, yes, I'm in favor of that."

"I'll tell you what," I said. "I'm ready to turn myself in. I've been a big drug pusher on the Lower East Side. If you let me out of here, I'll lead you to the people who supply my drugs. They're part of the mob."

She looked down at me, cocked her head a little, and said, "Oh?"

"Yeah, and I'll work a deal with you. Now I know

you don't want to follow me personally, but you can have someone else follow me when I go down there, and I'll lead them right to my connection. If there is a reward for those people—and I think there must be a big one—then you are going to get it, all of it."

She patted my hand and laughed, seeming to soften in her attitude toward me. "I guess I'll have to add that one to my list," she said. "You wouldn't believe all the different things I've been offered by people who want out of here. One girl offered me a million dollars. Another said she had connections and could see to it that I was named head of the nursing staff here at the hospital. One even promised me a husband. I turned her down. I already have one of those." Then she laughed.

"You think I'm kidding, don't you?"

"Well, let's not get into that right now," she said. "What I want you to do is to quit worrying about getting out of here. We have methadone, and we have various programs here that will really help you. And, young lady, you really need help."

"When do I get these straps off?"

"I talked to the doctor, and he said they can come off any time you're ready now. But I want to tell you that these wards are locked. If you try to escape and we catch you—and the chances are almost one hundred percent that we will catch you—then you go back to the straps again. So you see, it's up to you. Now if I take these straps off, will you promise me to be a good little girl?"

I nodded vigorously. I knew I was lying, and she probably suspected I was too. But I was willing to do almost anything to get out of those restraints.

After she unbuckled the straps, I wiggled my arms and legs and my fingers and toes and said, "Wow! You have no idea how much better that feels. You can count on me to behave."

For the first time since the accident I thought about Frank. Where was he? Why hadn't he come to see me?

"Is there a telephone I can use?" I asked.

"Sure, it's out in the hallway. But don't get smart with your phone calls. They're monitored too."

As soon as she left, I got up and walked around the room a little, gradually getting used to being up. Then I put on the hospital bathrobe they had furnished, went down the hall, and called Frank collect. When I told him where I was, he said, "Yeah, baby, I know all about it."

"How come you didn't come with me?"

"Hey, baby, I had all that stuff on me. I had to get back to the motel. But I found out where they were taking you and came by later that evening."

"You did? I didn't see you."

"No, they wouldn't let me in. They said they had you in the drug detoxification unit and that you couldn't have any visitors. They told me to come Saturday."

"When's Saturday? I've lost track of time."

"Two more days, baby. This is Thursday. Two more days and I'll be right there by your side."

I felt better already. Frank would have some idea about how to spring me out of this place.

"Frank, they've got me locked in here."

"I know. I talked with the people there. They said they have you in for observation. I guess they found out you are on drugs."

"Yeah, they know. They are giving me methadone so I don't get sick. But I still want out of here. It's almost like being in a prison. When you come on Saturday, be sure to bring my clothes with you. Okay?"

"Now, Denise, maybe you'd better just stay cool. They think you might have flipped a little. I told them you were all right—that you probably just banged your head in that accident."

"Frank, that whole thing's pretty cloudy in my mind. What happened at that accident?"

"I really don't know. You were right behind me in that traffic jam. The next thing I knew, I happened to look in my rearview mirror, and you started in reverse and plowed into the guy behind you. When I ran back there, you were unconscious. The police in the tunnel called the ambulance. I found out which hospital they were taking you to. When you came to at the scene, you were really cursing and screaming. I thought you'd flipped too. I've never seen you like that, Denise. It really scared me. It sure is good to hear your voice again."

"Frank, I can hardly wait for Saturday," I said. "And when you come, I want you to find a way to spring me out of this place. I'm counting on it!"

12

It seemed as though Saturday would never come. Just think! I'd be with Frank again. He always had the answers to my problems. This time he'd have a way for me to escape from this hospital.

When Saturday dawned, I fixed my face and my hair. I thought he might come in the morning. But when he didn't, I was sure he would be there in the afternoon. I knew he frequently worked late selling drugs and usually slept late in the morning. I assumed he would go and get some drugs and then come by for me after that.

But as the afternoon dragged on and Frank didn't come, I started to get upset. My mind went over all sorts of possibilities—including the fact that he might have learned who raped me and gone after Flip and Chuck.

Then I decided he must have felt it best to wait until evening, thinking it would be easier for me to slip out then. It would also be harder for anyone to follow us back to Jersey.

But when nine o'clock came and visiting hours were over and still no Frank, I was both mad and worried. So I went to the phone, called the motel, and asked for Frank.

"Is this Denise?" It was the motel manager who answered.

"Yeah. I'm at Bellevue Hospital."

"I know. Frank told me. But I have some bad news, Denise."

"Bad news?"

"Frank isn't here."

"Not there? Did he move? Where is he?"

"Last night the cops were swarming all over this place, Denise. They caught Frank with a lot of dope."

"No! No! Tell me it isn't true! You're lying!"

"I'm afraid it's so, Denise. I had no idea Frank was into that kind of business. I simply will not stand for dopers in my motel. No way. As far as I'm concerned, it's good riddance to bad rubbish!"

"Who ratted on him?" I screamed into the phone.

"Well, it wasn't me, Denise. I didn't know what was going on under my nose here. But I told the cops I'd be willing to cooperate with them in any way—"

"Why you dirty liar!" I interrupted. "You knew exactly what was going on, and you liked having me around for the convenience of your customers. I ought to—"

"It won't do you any good, Denise. Frank's gone now. I understand they have him in the slammer, and they'll be sending him away for a good long stretch. By the way, when you get out of the hospital, come around and see me. We might be able to work—"

I slammed down the receiver hoping the noise would break his eardrum. Then I started to bang my head against the wall. What was I going to do now? Frank was my way out of here, and the cops had him in jail!

I slowly walked back to my room, flung myself on the bed, and cried my heart out. I had to think of some way out of here, but I was in no mood to concentrate now.

I awakened the next morning still feeling sorry for myself. I began to assess my possibilities. Even when—and if—I got out of this place, where would I go? I knew it would be senseless to think of going home. As far as I knew, my mother hadn't even tried to find out where I was. She didn't care what became of me. She just didn't want me around. Frank wasn't around to help me. The only thing I could think of that I really wanted was to get out and get off again. But that would take money. And the only way I could make any money would be as a prostitute!

What choices! I was only sixteen—almost seventeen—and I had nothing to live for!

When the doctor came in that afternoon, I asked him when I would be getting out. His answer was a classic in evasiveness. Were they planning to keep me here indefinitely? Would they say I was mentally imbalanced and lock me up forever?

On Monday afternoon when the regular nurse came in—the one I had fussed at so much when I first came here—I told her that Frank had been busted. Then I started to cry and wailed, "What am I going to do? What will become of me?"

She sat on the edge of the bed, gently patted my arm, and said, "I know some people who might be able to help you. Have you ever heard of the Walter Hoving Home?"

"Walter Hoving Home? What in the world is that?"

"It's a home for girls located in upstate New York, in Garrison. The director's wife, Mrs. Benton, comes down here on Mondays and talks to the girls on this detoxification ward. She's been coming down here for a couple of years now, and I don't think I've ever met a nicer person. We have released a number of girls from here to go into their program. I don't know all they do up there, but they really seem to be able to help girls like you."

"Hey, I'm interested in anything that will get me out of this prison," I said. Then I saw her frown. "I mean, hospital," I corrected. "Anyway, I want out. That's no secret to you. What's this place again?"

"It's a home for girls who have been addicted to drugs or alcohol or who are delinquents and in trouble with the law."

"Like a reform school?"

"Oh, no. It's a Christ-centered program, and they have tremendous results. They seem to believe that all the girls' problems are basically what they call spiritual. You know, religious."

"Religious?" I said, laughing. "That leaves me out."

"I think it would be good for you to meet Mrs. Benton and talk to her a little about the program," the nurse said. "Even if you decide not to go there, you'll still enjoy chatting with her. She usually brings one of the girls from the home with her. Sometimes it's a girl who used to be here. It almost knocks me out to see the change in those girls!"

I stared at her in disbelief. "Are you putting me on?" I asked.

"No way," she replied. "This is the truth, Denise. And this Mrs. Benton's for real too. Do you want me to arrange for her to come in and see you? I saw her on the ward earlier today."

What did I have to lose? I wouldn't have any other visitors. And it made sense at least to find out what their program was all about. I had lost some of my enthusiasm when I found it had something to do with religion, but I could probably find a way to work around that!

I was leaning on my arm, staring at the wall that afternoon when I heard someone walk into my room. I rolled over and looked up into the biggest smile I have ever seen in all my life!

"Are you Denise?" she asked.

Her smile was so infectious that I smiled back without realizing it. Standing next to her was an attractive girl who looked as though she must be in her early twenties.

I sat up on the edge of my bed and said, "Yes, I'm Denise. And you must be Mrs. Benton."

She smiled again. "Yes, I am," she said. "But all the girls at the home call me Mom B. And this is Debbie."

I stuck out my hand to shake, but she ignored it. Instead she threw her arms around me, hugged me tightly, and said, "I'm so happy to meet you."

I wasn't used to being hugged, but I found myself putting my arms around that woman and hugging her too. There was something so powerful and magnetic—and motherly—about her. Why couldn't I have had a mother like her?

"Sit down," I finally was able to say to her. "I understand you have a place for girls in upstate New York."

"Yes, the Lord has given us a beautiful thirty-seven-acre estate in Garrison," Mom B said, settling comfortably into a chair. "Our girls come to us for a full year. While they're there, they learn how to live. And I mean really live. During that time, they study and work."

"Denise, we don't know much about you except that you've been having a drug problem," Debbie chimed in.

She was getting too personal! I'd put them off. So I said, "No, I really don't have a drug problem. It's really not much of anything. Certainly nothing to worry about."

"You know, Denise, I was once addicted to drugs,"

Debbie went on, ignoring my comment. "I had a really bad problem. I'd get on methadone for a while, then I'd go back on heroin. I was even pushing drugs."

I stared at her. She looked bright, smart, attractive, successful. There was no way she could have been an addict.

"Are you really off it now?" I asked.

Debbie threw back her head and laughed heartily. "Denise, I sure am! Not only am I off drugs, but I've found a real reason for living."

"What's that?"

"Jesus Christ!"

I'd never heard anything like that before. Oh, I knew that Jesus Christ was supposed to be a good man who lived a long time ago. Usually when I heard His name, it was used by someone who was cursing. I'd never gone to church that I knew of. But how could someone who lived a long, long time ago make any difference in the life of a person living today? That didn't make any sense at all. These people must be members of some weird cult—like those strange ones I'd read about in school.

"Since you said you wanted to meet us, Denise," Mom B said, "I guess you are interested in our program. Would you like to come up to our home?"

Both of them seemed to be anxiously awaiting my answer. Was I about to be their next victim? What was I getting into? I wanted out of this place, but not at the price of getting entangled in some weird cult. I'd better back off.

"No, I don't think so," I said. "I'm going to be okay. I can make it."

"Denise, you sound just like I did," Debbie told me. "You see, one of my problems was that I thought I was big enough to handle my own life. But everything I did messed up. When I started shooting dope, I told myself I was just going to shoot it to get high—you know, that good feeling. I told myself I could quit at any time. But I wanted that good feeling more and more. I didn't have to face life's realities when I was high. Then one day I had to get off just to get straight. That's when I realized I was hooked, trapped in a web of my own making. And then I got busted."

I had to admit to myself that this Debbie sure seemed to know what she was talking about. She'd been there. And her story sounded remarkably like mine. Maybe I was being too cautious. Maybe they really could help me, if they had helped her. And if it were a cult, I could still get out of it.

"How did you get into this home?" I asked.

"Well," Debbie said, "I was paroled and had a Christian parole officer. Since this was my first offense, he made the arrangements. God was good in letting me go to the home, Denise. There my life was completely turned around."

Were these people for real? I'd throw a problem at them that they couldn't handle.

"What would you do if you were raped?" I asked.

Debbie looked straight at me and said, "Denise, I know what I would do. I would forgive the rapist."

"Forgive?" I repeated in astonishment. "Not me! I'd like to see all rapists executed. I'd like to see them cut up into little pieces and thrown into the river for fish food. That's what I think about rapists!"

"I take it," Debbie said softly, "that you've been raped?"

"You'd better believe it—by two maniacs."

"Well, isn't that a coincidence," Debbie said. "It happened to me too. One day I did a very stupid thing. I decided to go down to the Lower East Side by myself. A

couple of guys grabbed me and dragged me down an
alley. I can't begin to describe all that happened."

I slid to the edge of my bed. "You were down on the
Lower East Side when this happened?" I asked.

Debbie nodded. "Two guys got me. I was high and
didn't offer much resistance. After that I went into
shock."

"You have been through that horrible, demoralizing,
degrading experience, and you're willing to forgive and
forget?"

"Well, Denise, the emotional pain is still there. I can
still remember the horror. But I can also honestly say
that when Jesus Christ came into my life and changed
me, His precious blood washed away all that bitterness
and anger. He completely took it out of my heart and
mind. And that had to be a miracle because before that I
wanted to see those two guys suffer the way they had
made me suffer! Since I've been born again, I've even
prayed for my attackers. I don't suppose I'll ever see
them again, but even if I do, the bitterness is gone."

I couldn't believe what I was hearing. Was it possible
that a person could be that forgiving? Was it possible
that a person could be hooked on dope and now be totally clean? Maybe there was more to this religion bit
than I was willing to admit!

"I'm not saying that didn't happen to you," I said
slowly, trying to find the right words. "But I know it
could never happen to me. My boyfriend wanted to kill
those goons, and the only reason I didn't tell him who
they were was that I was afraid they would kill him. But
I wanted them dead. I still want them dead. I have bitterness inside me that you wouldn't believe! I'm illegitimate. I just found that out a few months ago. My mother
hates me because I remind her of her evil past. And I
hate her because of the cloud she has put over my life.

Now the other day my boyfriend, who I've been living with, got busted for pushing drugs. They'll be sending him away for a long stretch."

Feeling a strong lump come up in my throat, I struggled to continue. Then the tears gushed out. "I have no reason to live!" I wailed.

Mom B was out of her chair and beside me in a second, throwing her arms around me and hugging me tightly. It felt so comforting, so reassuring, as though someone really did care what happened to me.

Through my tears I looked at her, and I realized she was crying too. So was Debbie! Can you believe it? Two people who a few minutes ago didn't even know I existed—and now they were crying along with me because of the heartbreak of my situation. There must be something to whatever it was they had!

Mom B patted my back and soothed, "Denise, you may not understand this, but I really love you and Debbie loves you. But even more than that, Jesus loves you."

"I don't understand," I replied, rubbing my eyes. "I have never done anything in my life that would make me worthy of anyone's love. I've done terrible things, things I'm deeply ashamed of."

"You don't have to be good for Jesus to love you," Mom B explained. "In fact, the Bible says that it was while we were still sinners that Jesus loved us. He loved us so much that He died for all our sins. Surely you've heard that Jesus died on the cross, haven't you? But He didn't die as a martyr, Denise. He died as a way of paying for all our sins and our guilt. It was sin that nailed Jesus to the cross—my sins, Debbie's sins, your sins, all the sins of everybody who has ever lived or ever will live on this earth. And because Jesus paid the penalty for our sins, God is able to forgive our sins. It was because He loved people so much that He did that, Denise."

What she was telling me seemed absolutely too good

to be true. "Do you think Jesus could really love some-one like me?" I asked. "I've been terribly bad."

"He already does love you, Denise," Mom B pointed out. "And He loves you just the way you are."

"But you really don't know what I'm like," I pro-tested. "I'm a junkie. I'm full of hate and bitterness. I've fought; I've stolen. I've even been a prostitute."

Mom B chuckled, and it surprised me. And it sur-prised me even more when she said, "You're no worse than I am."

"Did you do all those things too?"

"No. I was raised in a good home and went to a good church," she explained, "but I was still a sinner. There are no good sins and bad sins in God's sight. Sin is sin. And all people on earth have sinned. So even though I hadn't done all the things you have done, I still had to come the way of the cross—just as you do, Denise."

Debbie came over and put her hand on mine. "Den-ise, I did all those things that you say you've done. And I found out that Jesus loves me and died for my sins. He forgave me, Denise."

I could still see the tears shining in her eyes—eyes that were bright with hope and life; eyes that weren't pinpointed as a junkie's.

"Why don't you give Christ a chance in your life?" she asked. "I did it, and I've never been sorry. It has been the greatest experience I've ever had in all my life!"

I hadn't really thought about making a decision like this. Here I had been expecting to talk to two visitors about the possibility of entering a program and getting out of this hospital, and now they were asking me to make a decision which would change the entire course of my life. Was I ready for that? I didn't know. But I was aware of stirrings within me, and I was feeling good about what they were telling me. It made sense and gave me hope. Nothing had ever done that before. Maybe there was a way out after all!

So when Mom B asked, "Denise, would you like to receive Jesus as your personal Saviour?" I looked at her wistfully. Then she added, "I guarantee you'll never be sorry!"

What did I have to lose? Why not try it? If it did work, I'd find a way out of the hell I was living in.

"Yes, I would," I answered. "But I don't know how."

"Receiving Jesus is one of the easiest things to do in this world," Mom B explained, her smile seeming to fill her face. "People sometimes try to make it difficult. But you just listen carefully. I'm going to tell you about three steps."

She opened her purse, pulled out a little Bible, and said, "Here is a place to start; it's the Book of Romans, the third chapter, and the twenty-third verse. It says, 'All have sinned, and come short of the glory of God.' Have you ever sinned, Denise?"

"I sure have," I answered. "You know all those things I told you about. I've sinned like you wouldn't believe."

"Haven't we all?" Mom B responded. "There is something within us which confirms what the Bible says here, isn't there?"

I nodded. There was no question that I had sinned.

"Now let's look at another verse," Mom B said. "This one is in the first Book of John—near the end of the New Testament—the first chapter, and the ninth verse. It says, 'If we confess our sins, he is faithful and just to forgive us our sins, and to cleanse us from all unrighteousness.'"

I didn't quite follow, so I asked, "What does that mean?"

"It simply means that if we ask Jesus to forgive our sins, He has promised He will do it. Remember I told

you He died on the cross to pay the debt of our sins?
Well, because He did, He now has the power and authority to forgive our sins. But we have to ask Him to do
it."

"Do you mean that Christ will forgive all my sins?
You mean He really forgives?"

Mom B nodded, and Debbie chimed in. "I know it's
hard to believe, Denise. I had done some terrible, terrible things. But when I asked Jesus to forgive me, He did
it. And His forgiveness, the Bible tells us, means it is as
though it never happened! Can you imagine that? Every
terrible thing I've done in the past the Lord has forgiven
me! And I learned a Bible verse at the home that says
God will remember our sins against us no more forever!
In fact, the Bible uses the analogy that He takes our sins
and casts them into the depths of the sea. Denise, when I
asked Jesus to forgive my sins, He wiped the slate clean.
All my past was forgiven; my sins blotted out! And I
have a bright new future with Christ. You can have it
too!"

Could that be possible? I sure wanted to find out!

"Let's review a minute," Mom B suggested. "The first
step is simply for you to admit you are a sinner. The second step is to confess your sins to Jesus Christ and ask
Him to forgive you. And the third step is easy too. It is
just by faith to receive Christ. In the Book of Revelation,
the last book in the Bible, chapter three, verse twenty, it
says that Christ is knocking at our heart's door. If we
open the door, He'll come in."

"Denise, it's so simple that it almost seems like child's
play," Debbie added. "But believe me, receiving Christ
will be the most dramatic, dynamic experience that has
ever happend to you."

"Shall we go over the three steps again?" Mom B
asked.

"Yes," I replied. "I think I've got them, but I'm worried that I'm making it too easy."

"Didn't I tell you it was simple? And it really is. First, admit you're a sinner. Second, ask Jesus to forgive your sins. You don't have to name every one of them; just ask Him to forgive them all—and really mean it. Third, by faith receive Jesus into your heart."

I knew this sounded like what I needed. If it were true, it would indeed be the answer I had been searching for. But I was still a little skeptical.

"Denise, what I'd like you to do," Mom B said, "is to repeat this little prayer after me. In it we are going to acknowledge that you are a sinner, ask Jesus to forgive you, and then by faith ask Him to come into your heart. Are you ready?"

I still had some hesitation, but I nodded. At least I would give it a try.

"Lord Jesus, I confess to you that I am a sinner," Mom B prayed.

I repeated it.

"Forgive me of all my sins, every single one of them," she went on.

I repeated that too. So far so good.

Then Mom B said, "And by faith I receive You, Jesus, into my heart."

I repeated it. When I did, Mom B looked straight at me and said, "Denise, you pray your own prayer now, just like that one, only using your own words."

Hoping it would work, I said, "Jesus, I know I am a terrible sinner. You don't have to tell me that. I know it. And I'm sorry about it. Please forgive me of all my sins. And now I receive You into my heart. Please come into my heart, Jesus."

I lifted my head and looked over at Mom B, as if to ask her if I did it right. She said to me, "According to that prayer you just prayed, Denise, where is Jesus now?"

I thought a minute and said, "He's in my heart."

Debbie slapped her knee and exclaimed, "That's it, Denise! That's it! Jesus now lives within you. Remember, He said He would come in if you asked Him to. You asked Him, and He's kept His word!"

If that was it, how come I didn't feel any different? Debbie had promised this would be the most dramatic experience of my life, but I felt just the same as before I prayed.

I bowed my head and said tearfully, "I tried it, and it didn't work. I knew it wouldn't."

"What didn't work?" Mom B asked.

"When I prayed, nothing really happened. I didn't feel a thing. I'm still the same."

Mom B laughed. "No," she said, "you're not the same. But let me explain something. Everybody in the world is different. Right?"

I nodded.

"And because we're all different, we react differently," she went on. "Remember when you were a little girl playing with other little kids? If somebody gave each of you a glass of Kool-Aid, some kids would jump up and down for joy, some would squeal in delight, and some would just smile and drink it. Well, receiving Christ creates different kinds of feelings in different people. Some people have such a dramatic experience that it's like bells going off and lightning flashing. I guess that's how it was for you, wasn't it Debbie?"

"Oh, yes!" Debbie enthused. "I felt like a great weight had immediately been lifted from my shoulders, and I felt all clean and new inside!"

"Well," Mom B went on, "it doesn't always happen that way. It isn't at all unusual for someone to pray the prayer you prayed and then not feel one bit different. And that's perfectly normal too."

"It is?" I asked.

"Yes, it is. You see, the emotional experience—the feelings you talked about—has nothing to do with the reality, Denise. Remember I told you that the third step was to receive Jesus into your heart *by faith?* Faith means that you take Jesus at His Word. You believe He has come into your heart because you've asked Him to and because He said He would if you asked Him. That's faith—believing He does what He says He will do. As we walk with God every day, we have to learn that faith always has to come first. Feelings come later. Now, did you really mean what you prayed?"

"I sure did, Mom B. I tried to be as sincere as I knew how to be. I want desperately to have my sins forgiven and have Jesus living in my heart."

"Then, no matter how you feel, Jesus is living within you," Mom B assured me. "That's what the Bible teaches. You are saved, born again, a new creation in Christ Jesus because He is now within you and in control of your life."

"Remember, faith first, then feelings," Debbie repeated. "Later on you will know—I mean, have that real assurance—that it has happened."

Mom B and Debbie talked with me some more and shared some more Bible verses about what had happened to me. Then Mom B pulled a little pamphlet out of her purse and showed me a picture of the Walter Hoving Home. She told me again that the program was to help girls like me learn how to live life to the fullest by putting Christian principles into practice.

When she asked me if I'd like to come there for a year, I knew I would be the most stupid girl in the world to refuse an invitation like that. The place looked abso-

lutely gorgeous—even far, far better than the lovely little apartment Frank and I had shared.

Mom B left while Debbie chatted with me about the
home. She told me her reactions to it, how the program
had helped her, and that I would even be able to finish
my high-school education because they had a program
approved by the State of New York.

When Mom B came back, she told me, "I've made arrangements with the hospital for you to be released to
our care in a couple of weeks. They will reduce the dos-
age of methadone so that in two weeks you ought to be
clear. Then they'll evaluate your getting out. But I don't
think there will be any problem."

Getting out! The words sounded like music to my
ears! It was almost too good to be true. An hour or so
ago I didn't think I had a hope in the world. Now I had
hope! I was getting out!

The next Monday Mom B and Debbie visited me
again, bringing a Bible for me to study and giving me
some help in how to study it. They said that a new
Christian needs to study the Bible to grow spiritually.
They also helped me learn how to pray—just talking to
Jesus about the problems and difficulties I experienced
and asking His help in overcoming them.

The following Monday when Mom B and Debbie
came back, the hospital said I was ready to go with them
to the Walter Hoving Home. In one way getting out of
that hospital was like being released from jail. But it was
also while being confined there against my will that I
found the greatest freedom in all the world—freedom
from sin and the guilt of sin. For you see, Debbie was
absolutely right. As I studied the Bible and prayed,
gradually I knew that I was indeed a child of God, a new
creation in Jesus Christ. I knew my sins were forgiven
and that Jesus was living within me—just as He said He
would do.

I can't describe the thrill I felt as we entered that beautiful little bit of heaven known as the Walter Hoving Home. It was more gorgeous than the pictures. But more than that, I couldn't get over the wonderful feeling of the presence of Christ I realized when I walked into the main house. No one had to tell me. I knew Jesus was here. I knew that being a Christian was the greatest thing in the world and that God had exciting things in mind for me.

After I was assigned a room, received new clothes, and got acquainted with the other girls and the wonderful staff, I started the classes to learn how to live according to the Bible. We had classes in the morning, and a work-learning program in the afternoon. And I never did get over how much everyone there—girls, staff, everyone—cared about me and what happened to me.

It was great fun getting acquainted with Reverend Benton, whom we called Brother B. He preached to us every Sunday morning in chapel, and his sermons really helped me to see the possibilities ahead of me.

About a month after I went to the home, I got word about Frank. The cops had a mountain of evidence against him—both in New York and New Jersey. It looked as though he would probably get twenty years in the state penitentiary for selling drugs. His previous police record made the sentence almost mandatory.

I felt pretty down after hearing that. Other things got me down from time to time. I would be less than honest if I made you think that becoming a Christian meant I was living on one continual emotional high. Sometimes I would be so close to God that I wanted to go to heaven right then. Other times I would hit low points, feeling lonely and deserted. But I kept learning Bible verses that fit my situation exactly, and I was beginning to understand that God loved me and cared for me, no matter how I felt or what I was going through. And I realized He was always there to help me when I asked Him.

One of my greatest highs came after I went home on a weekend pass. My dad was back from Wichita; he couldn't find work there.

The first hour or so I was home was pretty difficult, to say the least. They all felt as though I had shamed and embarrassed them, and I really had. But as I explained to them how Jesus had changed me, they listened. I guess it was pretty obvious that I was a lot different person now than I was when I ran away from home. They had to admit that.

On Sunday morning they even accepted my invitation to go with me to church. Mom and Dad liked the services so well that they promised the pastor they would be back the next week!

Two months later Mom called me at the home. She was so overjoyed she could hardly contain herself. She and Dad had been going to church every Sunday since I had visited home, and that Sunday morning both of them had gotten saved!

It wasn't too long after that that Dagmar and Philip also got saved. It was almost too good to be true that a family like ours, such a short time ago rocked by dissension and bickering and hate, was now a Christian family showing love to each other!

My year at the Walter Hoving Home seemed like a two-week vacation. It was over far too soon. But my whole family came up for my graduation. You haven't seen such crying and laughing and carrying on as we did. I still can hardly believe the difference that Jesus Christ has made for us!

Because I was able to finish my high-school studies at the Walter Hoving Home, that fall I was able to enroll at Central Bible College in Springfield, Missouri. I'm studying to be a missionary—either to go to some country overseas and tell people how much Jesus loves them, or maybe I'll be a home missionary and go into a work similar to what the Bentons are doing in the Walter Hoving Home.

Frank? Well, he and I correspond now and then—but just as friends. I'm praying for him, that maybe somebody in prison will be able to reach him and fortify the message I've been trying to get across to him in my letters—that Jesus loves him and has a beautiful plan for his life if he'll just accept Him as his Saviour.

As I am here at Central Bible College, my thoughts are now going out to you. I don't know why you've taken the time to read my story. I have no idea where you bought this book. Maybe you got it on a rack in a bookstore. Maybe you picked it up at a grocery store. Maybe an interested friend gave it to you to read. Where you got it isn't important. The important thing is your relationship with Jesus Christ. Do you know Him as your personal Saviour?

Maybe you're like Mom B—a good girl raised in a good church. Maybe you're like me—messing up your life with drugs and prostitution and all sorts of evil. But it comes back to what the Bible says: "All have sinned." Everybody needs to know Jesus as the only One who can forgive sins.

Maybe you wonder about how it happens. I did. I didn't feel a thing when I first prayed. But I put faith ahead of feelings, and eventually I did have that assurance. I knew I was born again.

If you don't know Jesus as your Saviour, why don't you receive Him now? It really is simple—so simple that many people miss it.

Remember those three steps Mom B told me about? Well, let me repeat them.

First, just admit you are a sinner. You know you are.

Next, in a simple way, ask Jesus to forgive your sins. Tell Him you really are sorry for them.

Third, by faith receive Christ into your heart. Believe

that because He said He would do it, He will do it when you ask Him to. That's faith.

Why don't you just lay this little book aside right now, bow your head, and pray that prayer? Really mean it; don't just say the words. Jesus is waiting for you to pray it now. He loved you so much that He died on the cross for you. He longs to forgive all your sins, to wipe the slate clean—forever.

He wants to change you into a brand-new person who has something to live for.

Then why don't you drop Brother Benton a line at the Walter Hoving Home, Garrison, New York 10524, and tell him about your decision? He and Mom B and the wonderful staff and all the girls there are waiting to rejoice with you. And the Bible says the angels in heaven are waiting to rejoice over your decision too! Think of it! All of heaven gets excited when another person is born into God's kingdom!

You'll be rejoicing too. Because when you invite Jesus into your heart and life, you're a brand-new person with something to live for—like me!

The Walter Hoving Home.

Some good things are happening at The Walter Hoving Home.

Dramatic and beautiful changes have been taking place in the lives of many girls since the Home began in 1967. Ninety-four percent of the graduates who have come with problems such as narcotic addiction, alcoholism and delinquency have found release and happiness in a new way of living—with Christ. The continued success of this work is made possible through contributions from individuals who are concerned about helping a girl gain freedom from enslaving habits. Will you join with us in this work by sending a check?

The Walter Hoving Home
Box 194
Garrison, New York 10524
(914) 424-3674

Your Gifts Are Tax Deductible

Learn the Bible, challenge your wits, and have fun at the same time!

_____ **BIBLE CROSSWORD PUZZLES by Gretchen Whitlow** — A new collection of crossword puzzles and cryptograms for family enjoyment. $2.25

_____ **MORE BIBLE PUZZLES AND GAMES by M.J. Capley** — A vast assortment of puzzles and exercises, guaranteed to test any family's storehouse of biblical accuracy. $1.95

_____ **NEW BIBLE CROSSWORD PUZZLES #3 by Gretchen Whitlow** — A collection of challenging crossword puzzles and cryptoverses designed to inform, challenge and entertain. $1.50

_____ **NEW BIBLE CROSSWORD PUZZLES #4 by Gretchen Whitlow** — All new crossword puzzles. For use by families, church groups, travelers, and during your spare moments. $2.50